BLUE CASTLE

Sinners

MS. PAMELA

BLUE CASTLE
Sinners

TATE PUBLISHING
AND ENTERPRISES, LLC

Published by Tate Publishing & Enterprises, LLC
127 E. Trade Center Terrace | Mustang, Oklahoma 73064 USA
1.888.361.9473 | www.tatepublishing.com

Tate Publishing is committed to excellence in the publishing industry. The company reflects the philosophy established by the founders, based on Psalm 68:11,

"The Lord gave the word and great was the company of those who published it."

Book design copyright © 2015 by Tate Publishing, LLC. All rights reserved.
Cover design by Maria Louella Mancao
Interior design by Manolito Bastasa

Published in the United States of America

ISBN: 978-1-68187-343-5
Fiction / Christian / General
15.10.08

Oh Heavenly Father,

To imagine that you so wondrously painted the earthly skies and layers of galaxies, designed our planet's landscapes with colors arrayed since the creation and oceans from clear pastels to the darkest hues—only the one true living God—Elohim!

I am honored to have the privilege of this special assignment in the form of creative writing and blessed with the inspiration of your holy scriptures with their specific meaning and to share how countless their applications are for living this brief life. Thank you for considering an imperfect person to fulfill your perfect will.

All praises to you! Bless your holy name, Almighty Jehovah God—Elohim!

One of the daughters of the Tribe of Judah,
Ms. Pamela

"The Word of God is inclusive to all—Heaven is exclusive to all who hear His Word and obey."

ACKNOWLEDGMENT

Jalahh, your sticky notes, homemade cards and posters, I have them all! It's indicative of your excitement for us to succeed, especially when I was overwhelmed and burning both ends of this life candle.

My infamous "dream team," how much more love can I pour out?

Jaheesha, Jalahh, Jashawn, and Kaleb, your love, incessant encouragement, unending questions, and listening to me go on and on about life and God.

Talk about keeping me hard-pressed! Never forget the great mountain story.

A very special thank-you to my dearest longtime friend and sister saint-in-the-Lord, Ms. Bridget.

Remember when my laptop crashed? How resolute you were to check me on task, saying, "Finish the book!" and surprise me with a new one!

> "There are "friends" who destroy each other but
> a real friend sticks closer than a sister."
>
> —Proverbs 18:24

CONTENTS

TRADITION

Each year the week following Christmas, Pastor Anders Haugen, his wife Helen, and three children ventured off to their family vacation home. Helen, a native Californian, inherited the large four-bedroom cabin nestled away in the picturesque hills of South Lake Tahoe—two hours away from their home in Elk Grove, a Sacramento, California suburb. Helen's slender body and long legs kept her active in local and national swimming competitions. While growing up, she, her parents, and brother enjoyed summer boating and fishing, and during the winters, they snow-sled and skied at their favorite spots. Her only sibling, Adam, is a dairy farmer in Cody, Wyoming.

Pastor Haugen is the senior pastor at the Silver Rock Christian Center in Elk Grove. His natural blond hair and blue eyes, along with his tall and husky build, were the result of his Norwegian heritage. In the 1940s, his parents settled in Northern California from a tiny village outside of Oslo. He has two brothers living in the Los Angeles area, Nilas and Rasmin. His parents, who had since passed on, were devout Lutherans. Twenty-plus years ago, Pastor Haugen decided to leave the Lutheran church and seek out his own path to teach a simpler yet fundamental road to salvation. He has enjoyed a solid steady growth at the congregation over the years.

All three of their children—Peter, Andrew, and Sarah—were involved in the youth ministries. Andrew, a junior in high school, was taller than his father, and he played football. He bears the resemblance of Helen. Peter was born in January, and Sarah in December of the same year, and the two attended middle school. Sarah resembled her father and inherited her mother's swimming trait and competed locally. Andrew, meanwhile, ran track and was the family's techie whiz kid.

This was the time when the Haugens' schedules came to a halt, and they reconnected as a family. The pastor and his wife caught up on their reading, and they all took full advantage of the season.

"Thank you, Father, for another day! Time to get up, Anders, if we plan to leave around eleven!" said Helen as she stretched her arms from under the sheet.

"Morning, Helen. It's seven already. You've got to be kidding me."

"Good morning. Now you know I don't kid around about this vacation. It seemed to me when it was announced last night at church we would be away for our traditional week. Everyone realized they had to have a moment. We just stayed a little longer than we normally do."

"I know! But, sweetheart, that's the life of being a pastor."

"No. That's the life of being a good pastor. Now let's get up."

Helen rose and knelt on the side and began to pray, while Pastor Haugen also rose, walked toward the window, and stretched out his arms.

"Thank you Lord for another day!" he said in a soft voice.

Meanwhile in San Francisco...

As you drove up to 38661 Tierra Lynn Lane in the area of Sea Cliff, the plush foliage and the huge double ornate white glass stained doors symbolized the residents' wealth. The surrounding homes balanced privacy and sophistication as they were uniquely arrayed on the hills. The backdrop of the San Francisco Bay was spectacular, and layers of fog added to this mysterious ambience.

Daniel Piattoni is the owner of this palatial home for over seventeen years. Most referred to him as Dan. This six-foot tall, bronze toned, medium-built, fifty-five-year-old with salt-and-pepper clean-cut thick hair always had an abundance of dry humor, which he himself admitted from time to time was a tad off. Never married and no children, he spent a great deal of his time working from his home managing his real estate businesses. However, when time permitted, he was less than five minutes away from the Pacific Ocean where he would walk or sit, enjoying the tranquility of the magnificent waves. He worked tirelessly in the community on a couple of boards advocating for social issues of disadvantaged people and poor musically inclined students in San Francisco and the surrounding area. All the years of long arduous hours and lack of sleep, he slowly developed illnesses, and one in particular was multiple sclerosis.

In the spring, Cane Peters became his temporary houseguest and personal assistant. Cane was six feet, one and a half inches tall, extremely handsome with model-like features complemented with reddish blond hair and green eyes. Originally from Kentucky, his undeniable Southern accent always captured curiosity from others. He was hired part-time and did other odd jobs for Dan. Cane had become a dependable and trustworthy employee.

There was a knock at Dan's bedroom door.

"Cane, come on in and don't bother asking."

"And good morning to you too." Cane spoke from behind the door. He pushed the door open with his shoulder and walked in, steadily balancing a tray of tea.

The room was pale beige with white ornate crown molding. Hunter green drapes covered the east and south windows to complement the imported French mahogany bedroom set. To the west, a quaint fireplace was paired with a portrait of his mother, the late Mrs. Luccia Piattoni, hanging above.

The tea was steeping from a porcelain white and black rose teapot accompanied by dry wheat toast and his morning cannabis pill perfectly laid across the white cloth napkin.

"Morning. I don't know how good it was, but it's finally morning. No, seriously, I slept horrible and had an odd of sorts dream."

"Odd of sorts. Sorry to hear, but, Dan, I slept like a newborn baby. And I can't wait to get away from this place to smell some fresh mountain air."

"After this horrible night of sleeping, a few days in South Lake Tahoe will probably settle my mind. The dream was ghastly."

"Ghastly?"

"Never mind. I don't know why I bothered mentioning I had an awful dream to you."

"Okay. This morning is going south. Good morning, Sir Dan. So you didn't sleep well! Care to share? Take your green monster, and I'm sure you will feel better."

Dan stared in disgust as he swallowed the pill and sipped tea.

"All jokes aside. Please tell me about your dream. You know I have insight to meanings. Seriously!" he said while opening the drapes.

"I was lying stretched out in the freezing cold snow on top of warm money—literally hundreds, if not thousands, of bills. Snow was everywhere, and my hands were frozen. I couldn't move. I believe I wanted to feel the money, but I couldn't."

"Let me think about this one. Snow. Money. Hmmm."

"No, I'm not done. My mother always wore this signature perfume, and I could actually smell it. It was so real. I didn't see her, but just as I can smell this tea I'm sipping, I recognized an old familiar scent. How bizarre, don't you think?"

"Is your mom's birthday or the day of her death near?"

"No. Nothing like that."

"Hmmm. Usually when you dream about people who have passed on, it means you deeply miss them, requiring some type of closure, or you are going to hear from someone living that you've not heard from in quite a while."

"Cane, maybe it's a bad sign, and we should postpone this trip!"

"Postpone this trip! You've got to be kidding, right? This has been planned for some time. Did you eat something that didn't agree with you before you went to bed? You know that will do it."

"You know I rarely, if ever, eat anything before I go to sleep. Why even ask? Anyway, plans can be changed. Perhaps, in a couple of weeks we can make it up there."

"This is so unlike you. Is this because your mother was a part of your dream? People dream about deceased parents, children, and significant others all the time. It's only normal to reach back to pleasant memories. You are taking this as some sort of omen, and, furthermore, it makes you live by fear."

Cane sat in the window seat, peering out, and shook his head in disappointment.

"All right, Cane. Perhaps, you are correct, and I'm the last one to believe omens and that silly nonsense. South Lake Tahoe, here we come!"

"Man, you had me going there for a minute. I dream a conundrum of crap, and I say, oh well, and keep it moving! Next time, read a kid's book before you go to bed—*Hänsel and Gretel* or something."

"Out of all the books, why would you suggest *Hansel and Gretel*?"

"No reason. Just off the cuff, I guess. Why? Don't tell me you are superstitious about them too?"

"Of course not! Don't be silly. Would you mind reclosing the drapes, please? I need a couple of more hours of sleep, and it will make me feel better before heading up the mountain."

"I agree. Rested body, happy thoughts. I'll check in on you in a couple of hours. And I'm relieved you didn't change your mind."

As the door closed, he propped his pillows and curled into a comfortable slumber position. He regretted changing his mind to postpone, or even cancel, it all together. Deep inside, strong reservations about the trip lingered. Smelling his mother's favorite perfume scent was too genuine to dismiss. Lately, his mother weighed heavily on his heart, and how he longed for her.

And Cane was selfish as usual. He knew seeing all white in a dream is never a good sign, and yet he lied to me because he desperately wants to get out of the city to escape his own demons. Why did I once again cave into yet another situation that makes me uncomfortable? He said to himself.

Suggesting *Hänsel and Gretel* wasn't a coincidence either. One of his longtime and dearest friends, Ingrid, was possibly going to commit suicide one evening, and out of a gesture of desperation, he introduced her to the simplest of classical music, specifically *Hänsel and Gretel's* "Evening Prayer." Dan used the music to encapsulate the importance of everyone's life being boundless in purpose. When this brief enchanting melody of music was written, the composer's dream was for all who heard years after his passing to embrace its beauty. To this day, it was their binding secret, and when her spirit required solace, she would play the comforting piece.

What does all of this mean? Am I suffering from a paranoid anxiety disorder or overanalyzing a miniscule matter? he thought. Dan arose and walked toward the fireplace and opened a slender black tin box of matches and muses to light it—or not.

"Mom, were you here last night? Are you trying to tell me something? The Luccia House plans are coming along beautifully. A few details here and there to iron out, but *prometto il suo cortese e amorevole spirito non sarà mai dimenticato. Mai!*" said Dan as he rubbed the border of the portrait. He promised to never forget his mother's gracious and loving spirit. He lit a fire and sat down in the chair, and visions of this memorial project guided him into a gentle sleep.

Both men were in need of clarity and privacy to sort out thoughts and to formalize their individual future plans. However, this morning produced anxiousness for one and hesitance for the other.

Dan had traveled the world throughout his entire life. He bore witness to wealth and unspeakable poverty. His eclectic home displays were reminders of his global journeys with Aborigine art, Maasai masks, elegant Italian leather furnishings, and Persian rugs. However, the library served as a combination of social and academia gatherings. A black Fazioli piano belonging to his late Aunt Sovenia accentuated one corner.

Dan was once a Catholic, and now he was an atheist. As one who fully understood Christianity, he completely avoided any arguing or passing judgment on religious enthusiast. Most considered him brilliantly unusual with his acceptance and encouragement of others to practice any form of belief if it embraced peace and enlightenment. When he initially met troubled Cane, he strongly urged him to seek balance and meaning through reading the Bible.

Cane, a Christian with a Southern Baptist upbringing, sat quietly in the library reading his Bible as frankincense permeated the room. He hadn't stepped foot in a church since leaving Kentucky almost a year ago and yearned earnestly for the tradition he left behind. South Lake Tahoe was assuredly not Kentucky, but the majestic mountains and open air would suffice. There were moments when he felt completely in control of his life, and then out of nowhere, a word or something insignificant would produce an insidious behavior or bouts of rage. All the while, Dan believed time and patience were the healing balm.

Dan's late parents, Alonso and Luccia Piattoni, purchased the large property in the late fifties as an investment. They never accomplished the goal of selling or considered renting. Their free time was spent mostly abroad, and they vacationed in South Lake Tahoe on occasion. Year round, a local maintenance man kept the property, including a 1947 classic Chris Cruiser. However, when the Piattonis did get around to staying, it became one of Dan's favorite places. His mother called it the Healing Home. It was peaceful and free from any business distractions, and his father would proudly take over the kitchen and remind his mother that his cooking was what won her heart. Also, his father reminded Dan of how he anticipated seeing his grandchildren there one day. For Dan, this secluded tranquil property was one of nature's hidden jewels he appreciated and shared often with his close friends, especially Ingrid.

She believed with a serious conviction the place truly had healing powers. Dan remembered witnessing his mother sprinkling holy oil throughout the home and praying intensely. Sharing this childhood memory with Ingrid only strengthened her belief. She and Dan would drive up often in the summer, if only for a couple of days, to take in the splendor of South Lake Tahoe.

Two hours and fifteen minutes had passed since Cane had left upstairs. He assumed Dan would have awakened on his own by now. It was a little after nine, and driving to the mountains would take approximately four hours. Cane suddenly had an ominous thought, what if he changed his mind and decided to remain here and rest? He rushed up the stairs and nervously knocked.

"Dan! Dan!"

"Cane, come on in. Are we ready to head out?"

He opened the door and was astonished. Dan was fully dressed with two suitcases partially full with several manila folders and paper strewn across the bed.

"You got me this time!" said Cane. "I thought you were still in bed and contemplating postponing the trip."

"I told you earlier I wanted to rest a bit more, remember? I took a cat nap in the chair and decided to get up and make this happen."

"You started a fire!"

"I know. Don't say it. Why would I light the fireplace, and we're leaving? Impulse, I guess. Anyway, I phoned Selena, and she's stopping by in a couple of hours to check on things. I'm a bit hungry, and again I'm not. Are there any of those lemon scones left from yesterday?"

"Yes. I'll go and warm them for you."

"Thank you. Cane, are we set? Gas? Food? Snow chains?"

"Trust me. We are set and ready to go."

"Are you taking your laptop and all of those papers? That seems like a whole lot of work and no R and R."

"Yes. The Luccia House and other loose ends I need to tie up. No more procrastination."

"I'm sure this pet project of yours will be a success."

"No. Not mine, ours." Dan responded as he pointed to his mother's portrait.

Cane turned toward the portrait, looked inexpressively at Dan, broke a smile, and nonchalantly left the room.

"Good grief! Oh, well, that's Cane for you," he mumbled, shaking his head in dismay.

A short while later, Dan and Cane loaded up the black Range Rover and headed for the Bay Bridge out of San Francisco.

GETTING AWAY

Helen walked into the kitchen and heard TJ, their chocolate lab retriever, flop down the stairs.

"Oh, you know we're leaving too! Hello, boy! Oh, I love you too!" She gave him a brisk back rub.

"You want out? Out? No, not today!" She pretended to walk away, and TJ barked. She opened the back door to let him out.

Helen sat at the table while waiting for the coffee to brew and smiled, thinking of one of her favorite times of the year when she was peaceful, happy, and in a good place. She began to hum "These Dreams" by Heart.

Sarah walked down the stairs. "Morning, Mom. You're in a good mood. And what's that you're humming? I heard TJ. He obviously knows we're leaving too!"

"Good morning, Sarah. Yes, I'm in a great mood and so looking forward to getting away. And trust me, you don't know this old-school melody. These dre-a-a-a-ams! I have no idea why it keeps popping in my head. I'm in a good place, that's all. I was up most of the night prepping, and we're in great shape. Not much more to do. How's your packing coming along?"

"Actually, I'm almost done myself."

"That's a first."

"I'm excited and ready for snow like everyone else, I guess."

The Haugens one by one entered the kitchen and discussed their plans for the next few days. Helen prepared a hearty breakfast of sausage, omelet-like eggs, potatoes, and yeast biscuits. Her family maintained a healthy appetite and weren't finicky eaters, which made cooking an absolute pleasure. Through the school week, when everyone was done practicing their sports, expectations ran high for full course meals each night.

During this traditional vacation, all social devices were permitted with the exception of family meetings and outdoor activities. Also, church members didn't communicate with them. If there was an emergency, the Elders would contact Pastor Haugen. In the past, they'd only broken these rules a few times when someone passed away, and they needed him to minister or a hospital emergency. Pastor Haugen and Helen realized the years were fleeing, and they wanted to create family memories to last through the next generation.

An hour or so later, Pastor Haugen stepped away from the breakfast table and yelled up the back stairs.

"Okay, everyone! It's ten-thirty. We are pulling out at eleven o'clock sharp. Time to bring down your bags to the garage."

As he was yelling, the doorbell rang, and it was Mrs. Gilda Baines, their neighbor. The Baineses moved next door five years ago. Her husband, Nick, was a retired Air Force captain who did consulting part-time. Their two kids, Tatiyana and Justin, attended the elementary school in the neighborhood, and Sarah babysat for them on date night. The Baineses are Christians and attended a Baptist church in East Sacramento. During the summer, their kids attended a Bible camp in the sierras sponsored by Pastor Haugen's congregation. Both of these stay-at-home mothers would take walks together through the week, and Gilda was also an avid baker. Each year since the Baineses moved into the neighborhood, she would bake an extraordinarily delicious dessert for their annual trip to Tahoe. The Baineses kept an eye on things while they were away on vacation in case of any emergency at the house.

"Morning, Gilda!"

"Hey, Helen. Tradition, here I come."

"Oh my goodness, I'm so excited. Thank you. Thank you," Helen said as she led her to the kitchen.

"You are so welcome. Are you ready? It's a triple-decker German Chocolate cake."

"Morning, Gilda. Did you say German Chocolate?" asked Pastor Haugen.

"Uh-hum!"

"Oh, we love you!" said Pastor Haugen.

"Is Nick feeling any better?" asked Helen.

"Slowly but surely. Nick told me to tell you, Anders, if it wasn't for a shame, he'd keep the cake, which is his favorite, by the way, and run down the store and get you a chocolate cupcake. And I told him he'd better remain in bed with all those germs."

Everyone laughed.

"Gilda, we are so spoiled."

"I know, and I love it."

"Hello, Ms. Baines," said Peter.

"Hi, Ms. Baines," added Andrew.

"Hello, you two. Where is Sarah?"

"She's in the garage with Tatiyana and Justin," Pastor Haugen said.

"That figures."

"Wow. Look at that cake. What kind of cake is it?" asked Peter.

"Triple-decker German Chocolate," answered Helen.

"Ms. Baines, I assure you it will be gone by tonight," added Andrew.

"Enjoy the cake and yourselves. Leave all of your cares behind, and you know we'll be praying for traveling grace."

"Thank you for the prayers," said Pastor Haugen.

Gilda hugged everyone and then left, and Helen delightfully inspected the cake.

"Anders, now I feel guilty. She was up the night with Nick, and she made this cake. It's still warm. Can you believe it?"

"She's a gem."

Sarah was in the garage with Tatiyana, Justin, and TJ. Tatiyana was an aspiring singer, and Sarah played the guitar. She was always teaching Tatiyana new songs.

"Hey, kids! Listen, Sarah, time to get a move on. Pack it up," said Pastor Haugen.

"Okay, Dad. Sorry, Tatiyana. Gotta pack it up."

"Phooey!" replied Tatiyana.

The Baines kids hugged Sarah, and she went upstairs to complete packing.

"Andrew and Pete, I haven't heard a peep from either of you, which means you must be ready to go. Right? Right?"

"Sure, Dad," said Peter.

"Andrew!"

"I'm good! I'm good!" added Andrew.

"Dad, vacations mean relax and no shouting," said Peter.

"Honey, don't say a word. You know him. He's pulling your strings."

Helen tidied up the kitchen and reviewed her checklist.

"Did you remember to call Taylor's on Friday to clear the drive?"

"Sure thing. It's on the checklist. Jeez!"

"Sorry, honey. Have to make sure of these things."

Finally, the Escalade was packed to capacity with room for TJ in the back. TJ didn't do well with road trips. Out of necessity, they stopped a couple of times for the two-hour trip in order for him to take a breather and stretch his legs. After loading up, Pastor Haugen prayed.

"Heavenly Father, thank you yet again for another opportunity for us to take our traditional family vacation. We ask that you protect us and let no hurt, harm, or danger come to any of us. Please give us traveling grace to and from South Lake Tahoe. We are thankful for this blessing, which allows us to enjoy the activities of this season. We pray to be a blessing to others. It is in Jesus's name we pray, let us all say, Amen."

"Amen!" said the Haugenbunch.

Pastor Haugen, his family, and TJ took Highway 99 and headed for South Lake Tahoe.

THE GOOD DEED

Driving west on Highway 50 before they entered the Eldorado National Forest area, TJ began to whine with irritability. It was as if he knew they were at a halfway point. Andrew reached over the seat and rubbed his head.

"Okay, boy."

Traffic was actually more congested than usual. The snow was starting to really come down, and usually a little ways up, the California Highway Patrol required snow chains prior to driving through the mountains. Pastor Haugen took the next exit and stopped at a gas depot.

"I'm glad we left on time," Helen said.

"Everyone had the same idea we had," added Pastor Haugen.

He parked the Escalade, and the kids took TJ for a quick walk.

"Anders, we may need the snow chains before we get there."

"They're tightly packed in the rear corner just in case we need to get to them quickly. I've got this, Helen. Honey, I can't wait to sit by a fire, sip a nice cup of coffee, take in the smell of pine, and relax."

"We are all overdue some quiet time and fresh mountain air."

The doors opened.

"Wait a minute. Back already? What happened?" asked Pastor Haugen.

"Dad, TJ did his business, and I guess it's too cold for him too," said Peter.

"TJ, you know something we don't know," asked Helen.

TJ barked, and they all laughed. The lake and rolling hills of snow-covered ponderosa pine trees was a pleasing distraction from the traffic congestion, which caused a delay in their normal time of arrival. The house was five miles south off the main highway.

Finally, as they approached the bend in the road toward their home, they noticed two orange emergency cones in the back of a Range Rover parked just yards from their drive. The hood was up, and Cane was peering from the side.

"It looks like someone is having car trouble. I'll pull over."

Pastor Haugen parked in front of the vehicle. He, his sons, and TJ got out and walked over to see if they required any assistance. Dan opened the door and greeted the Haugens.

"Hi, there. It looks like you're having some trouble here."

"Yes, we called roadside service about forty-five minutes ago, and they said it would be a couple of hours before they could get to us. I believe it was a pothole a ways back, and it started riding funny. There was a loud noise, and then it stopped," said Cane.

"Bummer. This is our home, and we wanted to make sure everything was okay here."

"Thank you. I'm Cane, and this is Dan."

"I'm Pastor Anders Haugen, and my sons, Peter and Andrew."

Cane exuded a wide smile and reached out to Pastor Haugen with eagerness.

"Glad to meet you, Pastor Haugen. I'm a believer too."

"Are you?" Pastor Haugen asked Dan.

"No."

Peter interrupted.

"That's a really nice Range Rover."

"Thank you. I've had it for three months, and now it breaks down. What are the chances of that happening? I have a home ten miles up the road off Lamp Post Lane on Juliette Drive."

"Oh, I believe I know where Lamp Post Lane is," replied Pastor Haugen.

"Yes, the home has been in our family since I was a young boy, if you can believe that." Dan smiled.

"Here too! My wife, Helen, has been coming up here since she was a little girl. Small world, isn't it?"

"Definitely!"

"Listen. Once we unload and get situated, I'll come back and check on you two."

"No, you don't need to do that. We'll be just fine," replied Dan.

"It's no problem. It's freezing out here," said Pastor Haugen.

"Thank you, Pastor Haugen"

"Yes, thank you," said Cane.

Pastor Haugen and his sons returned to their SUV and headed up the steep tar-paved drive.

"Honey, the older gentleman, Dan, has a home on Juliette Drive off Lamp Post Lane. They ran over a pothole or something, and roadside service should be here in about an hour or so. That's what the young guy said."

"I know the area."

"Anders, it's so cold. Why didn't you invite them to wait with us until someone arrives?"

"Hold on, Helen. I told them that we would unload, get a little situated, and I would come down and check on them."

"Okay. Well, it looks like Benjamin did a great job clearing the drive and front. I'll call and let him know we made it in and thank him."

Benjamin Taylor owned a property management company in the area and also offered ground maintenance for the residents of South Lake Tahoe and the surrounding areas. During this time of year, the Haugens notified the company of their expected arrival date and time to schedule snow clearing in the drive and front porch.

"Thank you, God, for traveling grace," said Pastor Haugen anxiously.

"Yeah! Blue Castle finally," said Peter.

Pastor Haugen parked the Escalade, and TJ raced over his seat and jumped out as he walked around to open Helen's door. The house was refurbished ten years ago, and recently the furniture was replaced. This three-bedroom split-level home was near Lake Tallac with Sierra Nevada Mountain Range views. The spacious loft was an entertainment area with a pool table, big screen, telescope, and deck.

A "Welcome to Blue Castle" signage was located directly above the door. It was old and chipped with faded paint—just the way Helen preferred it. She helped her mother make the sign when she was four years old. Helen had a blue dollhouse and played with it near the edge of the water. One sunny day, the reflection reminded her of a castle, and she named it Blue Castle and told her mother their home was Blue Castle too. Later that day, Helen's father provided them with a piece of wood he cut and painted blue. Her father then hung the sign she and her mother made together. The Haugen kids from time to time spoke of how it was out of place and should be taken down, especially when the remodeling took place. Needless to say, this was always a hopeless request.

"Look, firewood ready to light and extra logs. What would we do without Benjamin?"

Pastor Haugen put down the luggage and lit the fire.

All groceries had been put away and the luggage in their respective rooms. It was an unbreakable rule to unpack before anyone was allowed to participate in any house activity or leave. In a militaristic fashion, the kids immediately made their beds and organized their items. Twenty minutes passed.

"Helen, I see Cane. I'm going down to invite them in. Andrew and Peter, come on. They may have a backpack or items to bring with them."

"Good. I'll make extra. Anyway, I prepped enough food before we left."

"Extra dinner?"

"You never know. It may be another hour before anyone arrives. It's fine."

"It's up to you. You're the boss!"

Sarah smiled. Pastor Haugen, the boys, and TJ headed down the drive. The temperature had dropped, and they were both now seated in the Rover. Dan rolled the window down.

"Hey there, you two. Any word?"

"I spoke to roadside service, and unfortunately it may be a little longer than we anticipated. Not only is this the time of year when they're extremely busy, but they are short-staffed. We have to wait our turn."

"Well, wait your turn with us. The two of you are invited to join us in our warm home out of the cold. Helen is preparing an early dinner, and we have more than enough if they don't show up before it's ready."

"Are you sure? We do not wish to cause any inconvenience," asked Dan.

"Come on. We're distant neighbors."

Dan and Cane looked at one another, smiled, and exited the Rover. Dan took the briefcase, and Cane got his duffel bag.

"And who are you?" Cane asked TJ.

"That's TJ. You'll never find a happier dog on the planet," Andrew replied.

"As cold as it is, your food items should be okay."

"Thank you again, Anders."

As Dan approached the home, he noticed the antiquated sign, "Welcome to Blue Castle," and he laughed.

"I know this isn't much of a blue castle. Let Helen tell you the story behind that."

"Oh no, Pastor Haugen, I wasn't laughing at the sign per se. It reminded me of something else, that's all. I like it just the way it is. It adds character to the place."

"Mom will like you for saying that," added Peter.

Andrew held the door open.

"Thank you."

"Thank you."

"Helen and Sarah, we have guests."

They both left the kitchen area.

"Hello, ma'am. I'm Cane Peters, and this is Dan Piattoni."

"Nice to meet you both. This is our youngest, Sarah."

"Hello."

"Cane, where are you from originally?" Helen asked.

"Kentucky."

"Beautiful accent."

"Thank you."

"Dan, are you from the area?"

"Yes, I'm originally from California."

"It's a shame it's taking so long for someone to come and see about your Range Rover."

"It's the holidays and one of the busiest times of year, I suppose."

"Well, Dan and Cane, please relax and enjoy the nice fire," Helen said. She and Sarah returned to the kitchen to continue preparing dinner.

"Thank you again for inviting us in," Cane added.

"Would either of you care for a fresh cup of coffee?" Pastor Haugen asked.

"Thank you much. I'd love a cup."

"No, thanks, for me, sir. It feels so much better in here," Cane replied.

Pastor Haugen prepared a fresh pot of coffee and served Dan. TJ lay out by the fire as Cane and the boys went upstairs and played with the PS4 game station. Dan shared with Pastor Haugen how he and his father would fish and take their 1946 Classic Chris Craft boat for lake cruises and that the boat was in mint condition stored at a facility in Tahoe. Pastor Haugen was enthused by his late father's toy, and Dan extended an open invitation for him to see it at his leisure when the weather changed. Both revealed their deceased parents were immigrants and very spiritual.

Dan took an interest in Pastor Haugen's missionary projects specifically—how they were developed, managed, among others.

THE LIE IN TRUTH

Still no word from roadside service, and it was now time for dinner.

The aroma of the artisan bread and a hint of Mrs. Baines's German Chocolate cake permeated the home. The Haugens and the two new guests gathered anxiously at the table to eat Helen's famous garlic shrimp and chicken pasta with tomato and zucchini salad. This meal was one of the family's favorites, and she prepared it always during their stay. The oversized man-made oak dining table comfortably seated everyone. After the home was remodeled, a local artist made the table especially for the Haugens. A floor-to-ceiling bay view window was added, which served as an excellent backdrop to the picturesque Sierra Nevada Mountain Range.

"Helen, it looks as though you've outdone yourself again." Pastor Haugen boasted.

"I made more than enough. When the two of you leave, please take some with you for later."

"Thank you, ma'am." Cane nodded agreeably.

"That's really thoughtful of you, and I will hold you to that," said Dan.

Pastor Haugen, sitting at the head of the table, reached his left hand out to Sarah and then his right to Cane. Cane smiled eagerly with anticipation and held Anders's hand, and Dan discreetly noticed.

"Let's bless the food. Dear gracious and merciful Heavenly Father, we are so thankful for this food prepared by Helen and Sarah. And thank you for our guests we are sharing this meal with. Please bless this meal. In Jesus's name, let us all say, Amen."

Everyone said Amen with the exception of Dan. Helen noticed and politely smiled at him.

"Guests first!"

"No, sir. You don't have to. It's okay," responded Cane.

"Son, you are our guest."

The food was patiently passed on to the guests from one end of the table to the other, and now all were delighting in the succulent meal.

"So, Cane, you said you're from Kentucky. How long have you lived in California?" asked Pastor Haugen.

"Not long at all. Not even a year."

"We were so busy talking about boats and our parents. Are you related?" asked Pastor Haugen as he looked toward Dan for a response.

Dan took a bit of bread and shook his head.

"No, we are not related. I met him when I came out here."

"Okay, I see. It's a blessing to meet good people in a strange city."

"Yes, it is. Everyone needs help now and then," said Dan.

"What do you do? Are you in school?"

"No, I'm not in school. I've been working odd jobs and assisting Dan until I land something permanent, I guess. Trying to get it together!"

"It takes a lot of fortitude to leave your hometown. My parents moved to this country from Norway when they were young. It was difficult for them, but they survived it and did well for themselves. They were hard workers and struggled, but somehow managed to put my two brothers and me through college. God first and having a good education was right up there."

"My parents raised me the same way. All I ever heard was education and having your own business," Dan added.

"Amen. All I ask of these kids is to do their best and let God do the rest. I heard you tell Anders your parents were immigrants too," asked Helen.

"Yes, they were from Italy. They passed away some time ago."

"I know that feeling," said Helen.

"Yes. Sorry, Dan. I miss my folks sorely, but they are in a much better place," added Pastor Haugen.

"And absent in the body, present with the Lord," simultaneously says Pastor Haugen and Cane as they laughed.

"Cane, so you are a Christian!"

"Yes! My father is a pastor back in Kentucky. Very busy congregation. I was telling Andrew and Peter I worked with youth ministries forever."

"Amen! And you left your roots to come out here all alone?"
He nodded.

"Hmmm. All of my kids are in the youth ministry. That's wonderful. I knew there was something special about you. Have you found a church home?"

"No. Not yet! Sometimes people need a change and have to do things on their own."

"Oh, I know about that. Don't we, Helen?"

"We sure do."

"My parents were Lutheran, and about twenty years ago, I began my own work. The journey was not without its challenges, but it has been rewarding."

"Amen, Anders."

"I pray that you find what you're searching for and locate your church home soon. It's important to be connected with other Christians. It's one way of keeping you grounded, son."

"I know, sir, and I plan to."

"Dan, so you aren't a Christian?"

"No, I'm not."

"Well, we will be praying for you, and I'm sure Cane is a source of encouragement."

"I plan to do my best and do right by Dan."

"So do you guys live in the city or outside? I know the area quite well. I was born in Oakland," asked Helen.

"We live in Sea Cliff."

"Oh my goodness, Sea Cliff! That's an affluent area, and some of the wealthiest people live there."

Dan humbly smiled.

"Now I am curious. Who are we in the presence of?"

"No, it's not that serious. My parents made sound financial decisions that afforded me this lifestyle. At the end of the day, it's only money, wouldn't you say? It can buy you everything but health. Right?"

"Well, it was a blessing we were there at the right time to assist you and another excuse for Helen to prepare more food. However, we are indulging in a triple-layer German Chocolate cake, compliments of our neighbor, Mrs. Gilda Baines. She makes us a special dessert for this trip each year." He patted his stomach and laughed. "You can't leave without tasting some of it."

"So you make a trip here each year?" Dan inquired.

"Yes. Every year after Christmas, we leave Elk Grove and come here until New Year's Eve," replied Pastor Haugen.

"Ms. Helen, this has to be one of the best meals I've enjoyed since leaving Kentucky."

"Why, thank you, Cane!" She mimicked with a Southern accent.

"Cane, did you ever go to the Kentucky Derby?" asked Sarah.

"Are you kidding me? Every year!"

Cane spent the better part of ten minutes describing the horses, lady's hats, and events surrounding the derby. The meal ended, and desert vanished as quickly as it was served. The descriptive Southern tales lured the curiosity and interest of the Haugen family and Dan.

Dan especially took note since Cane had never revealed this side of himself. A new jovial and content Cane appeared—not the intense and convulsive one he'd known.

A couple of times, Dan noticed Cane made statements with an arrogant posture and deliberate eye contact to him, as if to say, "This is who I am." Dan mused, one thing was for certain, he missed Kentucky and was borderline intolerant of where he was now.

"Wow, Cane. I couldn't leave all my family and move to another place leaving all that behind. I'd be so sad," Sarah added.

Cane looked at Sarah, and his countenance changed from merriment to a stoic glare.

"Son, Sarah didn't mean to make you homesick. It's okay. That's why there's Skype and cell phones. Not to mention an air ride away," said Pastor Haugen as he pated Cane's arm.

"Yes, Cane, you're only a call away." Dan reiterated.

Cane looked at Dan, slightly astonished by the comment, and Helen noticed it all.

"You talk to your folks regularly, don't you?" asked Helen.

"Not really!"

Silence was declared, and Sarah looked at her dad.

"I'm sorry, Cane," Sarah said in a low voice.

"No worries. Soon! You just enjoy your wonderful family, young lady," Cane replied.

"We are here on our vacation, and no time for bluesy-whoosy. Helen, I will make a fresh pot of my special coffee while Dan and Cane relax and let your good cooking settle in."

"Sounds like a plan," said Dan.

Helen and Sarah began clearing the table, and the others walked over to the living area. Cane stood, admiring a dated family portrait, and Dan joined him.

"Cane, I don't ever remember seeing you this blissful. Yes, a tad blissful. Maybe this trip will do not only me some good, but you too."

He attempted to pat Cane on the back, and he rudely walked away without saying a word. The rude gesture irritated Dan. All the while, Helen took notice. Dan's phone rang.

"Great, I think it's the tow company," Dan muttered to himself as he answered his phone. "Hello. Speaking. No! I asked that you call me fifteen to thirty minutes prior to arrival so that we could meet you there. That's unacceptable. Let me speak to your supervisor. You are the supervisor. Four to six hours! We're talking about past eleven. I'm tired, and this is an inconvenience. Why didn't someone just call as I requested? I understand you being short-staffed and all, but this is a major inconvenience. First thing in the morning is fine. What choice do I have? Again, please call me at least fifteen to thirty minutes at this number. Thank you."

"Now what?"

"I guess you heard. They never called, of course, as I requested. When they arrived and found my car vacant, they left to another call out the area. And to top it off, they're short-staffed. Pastor Haugen, if it isn't too much of an inconvenience, would you please take us to my home? I know it's about twenty-five minutes away. We would sincerely appreciate it. I will generously compensate you."

Pastor Haugen looked at Helen.

"Dan and Cane, I don't trust these conditions, and I'd feel comfortable waiting until the morning. I'm sure it's all right with Helen if the two of you stay here for the night. You certainly aren't going to sleep in the Rover, and there's no way I'm going to send anyone out in this weather."

"I was going to call a cab," replied Dan.

"Really?" added Helen.

Everyone laughed.

"Are you sure? I'm sure I can speak for Cane as well and say we don't want to cause any inconvenience on your family vacation."

"It's not a problem. Morning is better, anyway. You'll be rested and ready to deal with whatever the day offers," said Helen.

"Thank you so much," responded Cane.

"I have extra everything—toothbrush, combs, blankets, you name it."

"Then it's settled. Just relax and enjoy the rest of the evening with us," said Pastor Haugen.

"Pastor Haugen and Helen, thank you. I will not forget this! And to be honest, I am a bit tired from this day. Please allow me to compensate for everything. You've gone over and beyond," Dan added.

"Taking your money is an absolute insult, and it isn't necessary. God is always blessing us," said Pastor Haugen.

Cane hugged Pastor Haugen. Dan shook his hand, and Pastor Haugen hugged him.

"Now that's settled! Anyone care for a cup of my special coffee?"

"You guys relax, and the kids and I will get the rooms squared away. Take in the evening's spectacular view," said Pastor.

"Andrew, would you get some more wood? The fire is getting low."

"I'll get it, Pastor Haugen. Where is it?" asked Cane anxiously.

"It's right outside the kitchen door to your left. Thanks, Cane."

It was close to ten o'clock, and the entire household was winding down. The play station had occupied Andrew, Peter, and Cane, while Sarah's interest was a game on her iPad. Pastor Haugen and Dan engaged in small talk mostly regarding South Lake Tahoe and the changes over the years. Helen was in the bedroom comfortably curled on the bed, reading one of the books she brought up.

Dan's irritability with Cane heightened with his earlier loftiness, and he did not recognize Cane. He was relaxed, laughing, and in his comfort zone. For a moment, he wondered if he was bipolar and thought, no, he would have identified traces of this behavior early on. Cane was, for this brief moment, living vicariously through this family; he deeply longed for them. No need to cry and scream, "I miss my family." It was too revealing to deny. It was as if Cane purposefully wanted Dan to witness his afternoon of jubilation with the Haugens—"See me as I am and not as a puppeteer in your controlling world."

Dan should have shared Cane's ability to finally be happy among a familiar setting, but instead, an embittered attitude was seeping like an eruptive chemical experiment. He was recalling how he welcomed him into not only his home but also his inner circle of some of San Francisco's prominent and affluent people. Though his friends considered him extraordinarily rude and evasive, yet, to think without fail, he defended his behavior and attributed it to being in an unfamiliar place. However, the fat lady was singing, and the lie in this truth was over.

Pastor Haugen came from the bedroom.

"Helen and I have been talking, and here's the setup. Sarah, you bunk in with your mom, Andrew you with Peter, Dan and Cane, you can take Andrew's room there, and I will take the sleeper sofa."

"Dad, Pete and I can take the sofa."

"Your mom and I knew that was coming, and the answer is no. You think your old man can't live the rough life from time to time? Think again, son," he said, laughing.

Andrew responded with a dubious look.

"Dan and Cane, Helen will be out shortly to get you two set up. I hope it's not a problem for the two of you men bunking together?" He smiled.

"It won't be. We both are gay," said Dan as he looked at Cane.

"I beg your pardon?" asked Pastor Haugen.

"We are both gay, and us bunking together won't be a problem for either of us."

Motionless was everyone in the house, including Helen who was standing in the doorway. Dan conceitedly looked at Pastor Haugen, knowing the statement had him staggered. Cane's eyes locked with Helen, and he bowed his head in a wounded jolt. Within seconds, all eyes were frenziedly drifting, and finally in that very moment, they succinctly arrived at Pastor Haugen.

"No, we aren't lovers, but we are friends who happen to be gay, I guess you would say. This shouldn't be a problem, right?"

"The both of you are gay? All the time you are here in our home and not one word or mention that you are gay except for now!" Pastor Haugen responded in an elevated voice.

"Is there a problem?"

"You…" Then he paused. "Oh my dear God. Yes, there is a problem here. Oh, yes. We are Christians, and we don't believe in homosexuality. It's a sin against God."

Helen walked over and stood next to her husband.

"You two enter our home as though you were normal men, and you have the audacity to ask, is there a problem? You damn right there is."

"There is no need to get into a spiff about something that is natural and normal. A sin against God is open to interpretation," replied Dan.

Pastor Haugen was upset and looked at Helen as he placed one hand in his pocket and his fist on his mouth. He looked at Cane.

"You know, Cane, I can understand this unbeliever, but you… you've convinced everyone in my family that you were a Christian. Your dad is a pastor, and with all of your upbringing and his teachings end up here like this. Are you perpetrating? What's going on with you?"

Cane resorted to a subservient posture and shook his head, saying not a word, only a hard sigh.

"For the record, I'm not an unbeliever. I'm an atheist. We have a huge difference here."

"Dear God. You are a homosexual atheist? If this isn't the bottom of the barrel, I don't know what is."

"Pastor Haugen, when I first met you, you asked if I was a Christian, and I said no, remember? That is the truth. Furthermore, there are gay Christians all over the place. What's the big deal?" Dan said flippantly.

"It's a major deal and not in my house. And furthermore, true Christians are not gay because they know what the Word of God says about unnatural affection and its consequences. It's an abomination to the Almighty."

"That type of believing is for Cane. I don't believe in God, which means it does not apply to me."

"Oh, Jesus!" Helen shouted as Sarah approached and rubbed her back.

"I'm so, so sorry for all of this," Cane said as he angrily looked at Dan, who mumbled, "Whatever."

Sarah, for a split second, looked at Cane and was crushed at the revelation of him being gay. Her eyes no longer were bursting with enthusiasm of hearing about life in Kentucky; she was disappointed.

"Being gay is not the end of the world. Jeez," added Dan.

"You and your nonchalant attitude toward God is pushing me to the limit here. I'm doing my best to remain civil and conduct myself in a Christian manner for the sake of my wife and kids. You can get off your homosexual soapbox right here because this conversation is over. Your up-close and personal moment with this family, as I said, is over. Homosexuals push for this, push for that. Have you ever stopped to ask yourself why there are so many complications with this perversion?"

"I'm sure you will enlighten me on perversion one-o-one."

Peter whispered to Andrew, "Man, he flipped the script on us," and Andrew nudged him.

"Downplaying perversion will not change the severity of you choosing that lifestyle. I'll tell you why, and the both of you need to hear this. It's against the natural order of God. God's plan flows perfectly with a natural rhythm, a natural cycle. I'm talking about the ocean currents, our food, and the seasons, and we are his masterpiece. Yet, every recorded action by man when he attempts to disrupt that flow—I don't care what it is—produces adverse consequences, disruptions, destructions, and distortions. This includes unnatural sexual acts beyond Sodom and Gomorrah."

"Here we go. I knew this was coming. I wondered when you were going to bring up the old Sodom and Gomorrah."

Pastor Haugen's spirit calmed as he looked at his family. Helen and the kids were watching his every move, and as tempting as it was to attack this unbeliever, he needed to exercise restraint and reel in his emotions and stand on the Word of God.

"Oh, no, my friend. The disobedience to God went further than Sodom and Gomorrah. The scientific proof of this continuance of disobedience to God is being viewed by thousands every year. It's a pillar of salt. Once, a living and breathing female whose curiosity to see the sexual perverted cities destroyed cost her her life."

"Everyone is entitled to their beliefs and nonbeliefs. Before I told you we were gay, everyone in here was cordial and inviting toward us. Now it seems you treat us with disdain, or even worst, that you are somehow better than us."

"Dan, that isn't true at all. We don't think we are better than you. We think higher of the Word of God," added Helen.

"Being gay doesn't equate to being less than or evil," Dan responded.

"Please don't twist our words here. I'm simply saying Satan has manipulated that culture. Case in point, take the rainbow you so arrogantly wave. After the great flood with Noah, God made a covenant with man that he would not destroy the earth by water ever again, and it was sealed with a great rainbow. Today, a rainbow symbolizes homosexuality. I'm sure whoever began that trend did not have the covenant in mind—another abomination."

> And God spake unto Noah, and to his sons with him, saying, And I, behold, I establish my covenant with you, and with your seed after you; And with every living creature that is with you, of the fowl, of the cattle, and of every beast of

the earth with you; from all that go out of the ark, to every beast of the earth. And I will establish my covenant with you; neither shall all flesh be cut off any more by the waters of a flood; neither shall there any more be a flood to destroy the earth. And God said, This is the token of the covenant which I make between me and you and every living creature that is with you, for perpetual generations; I do set my bow in the cloud, and it shall be for a token of a covenant between me and the earth. And it shall come to pass, when I bring a cloud over the earth, that the bow shall be seen in the cloud: And I will remember my covenant, which is between me and you and every living creature of the flesh; and the waters shall no more become a flood to destroy all flesh. And the bow shall be in the cloud; and I will look upon it, that I may remember the everlasting covenant between God and every living creature of all flesh this is upon the earth. And God said unto Noah, This is the token of the covenant, which I have established between me and all flesh that is upon the earth. (Gen. 9:8–17, KJV)

"It's not an abomination, but our symbol of who we are, like an insignia. Now you've got it twisted."

"An insignia?"

"God in heaven knows we no longer use the word *gay* in the same sentence as we used to. Where is it going to end?"

"You see it as the glass half-empty, I half-full. It's prospective."

"This NGP aka New Gender Plan is nothing new under the sun, and it too will have equal, if not more severe, consequences than Sodom and Gomorrah," said Pastor Haugen.

"The NGP—now that's a first for me!" said Dan.

"The only difference between Bible times and the NGP is that there are now legalities attached. Nothing new," added Pastor Haugen.

"Cane, you have nothing to say about any of this?" asked Helen.

"No, ma'am. Right now, I think it's best I remain quiet. I will say that I'm sorry to have disappointed everyone and caused such friction," Cane said as he looked on contemptuously at Dan.

"Understand me, Dan and Cane. I am not here to condemn, but to save."

> For God sent not his Son into the world to condemn the world; but that the world through him would be saved. (John 3:17, KJV)

"Dan, I'm done, and we're not about to go in circles all night. I know we will be praying for the both of you. It's getting late, and since we are all here for the night, here are the new sleeping arrangements. You take the room, Dan, and, Cane, you take the sofa sleeper. I'll take the sleeping bag on the big bear. That's it. That's final," Pastor Haugen said in a stern voice.

"In the morning, the tow service will be here, and you can go on with your lives literally. We are Christians, and I'd prefer to maintain company with like-minded people. I trust I've made myself clear."

Pastor Haugen looked at Cane.

"I understand, sir," said Cane.

"Not a problem," Dan added. "Helen, I'm truly sorry. Please know that it was never my intention to upset you or your household. Please believe me."

She softly smiled.

"I'll get the extra blankets and pillows out the linen closet, along with toothbrushes and wash towels."

"One of you boys let TJ out before we lock up," said Pastor Haugen.

Andrew and Peter gathered items and headed for the bedroom with TJ. The well-mannered young men became sidesplitting juveniles—Peter energetically dived on the bed, and Andrew lay prostrate on the floor.

"Snap!" said Andrew.

"Oh my God, what the heck just happened here?" asked Peter.

"Unbelievable!"

"And Cane's a f-a."

"Shhh! Be quiet before someone hears you. You know dad despises that word. I can't get over Cane. He's frickin' gay. Oh my God! Did he seem gay to you?"

"How do you expect me to know? Bro, this is insane."

"He was ticked off at Dan for telling too!"

"Ah, man, I picked up on that one. He probably didn't want us to know. Do you think that's why he left Kentucky?"

"Undercover! How the heck do I know? Let's ask him!"

"He's probably undercover. He couldn't hide being PO'd at Dan."

"Ah, man, old school didn't care. A gay atheist."

"Unbelievable! What do you think some of the people at church would say when they hear? Oh yeah, 'The Haugens had a gay couple spend the night with them.'"

"Sir, that's going to go over very well, I'm sure."

"Dang!"

"This is messed up. Why was Cane just standing there?"

"And why do you keep asking me the same question over and over? I don't know."

"He was all happy and seemed so cool."

"I guess now we'll have a Bible class on gay etiquette if they're your houseguest. Ask first!"

They both laughed.

"Wow! We better keep it down. It won't be funny to Dad."

"Who are you telling?"

"It' all good. It will be over in the morning. At least, they aren't outside somewhere freezing to death."

"Man, I'm tired. You taking TJ out?"

"I guess. Come on, boy."

Andrew nonchalantly took TJ through the kitchen out the back door.

Pastor Haugen's family witnessed their father proudly proclaim the Word of God. Yes, strangers were in their home as strong and opinionated conversations ensued. It could have easily escalated into a disastrous night if he hadn't exercised control and confidence in balancing this fragile situation.

MUSING

Restless slumber awakened Sarah. She quietly sat on the edge of the bed, looking back as not to disturb her mother. Replaying the bitter dialogue between her father and Mr. Piattoni kept her awake. Sarah was worried about her dad. She carefully sat up, robed, biting down on her lip and tip-toeing to the door and grasped the knob securely. The door made a soft pop, and she exited. Her father was seated at the kitchen island, sipping from a cup.

"Dad!" she called in a whispering voice.

"Sarah, what are you doing up?"

"I should ask you the same."

"You should go back to bed."

His eyes were red and swollen from crying.

"Dad, what happened to your eyes? What's wrong? Do you want me to get Mom?"

"Shhh. Keep your voice down. No, I'm fine."

In whispering voices, they continued to talk.

"Those two really upset you, huh?"

"I'm fine, baby girl. I told you I'm okay."

Sarah squeezed his shoulders.

"They seemed at first to be all right. We didn't know they were gay. Dad, I hope you are not blaming yourself for any of this. You're a good person. Look at it like this, in a few hours, it will be all over, and we can continue with our tradition, right?"

"You are so right."

"I'm thirsty for a glass of water."

He smiled as she quenched her thirst and pulled up a bar stool next to him.

"Why don't you go back to bed and try and get some shut eye?"

"No can do. I know you've been praying, and I just want to keep you company."

She pushed her father with her shoulder.

"Come on. I'm just like you, and I'm not going anywhere."

"It did get a little messy here earlier."

"Dad, Cane said he was a Christian, and he wears a cross. He didn't seem gay to me, but then I don't personally know any gay Christians to compare him to."

"Well, the blessing is we met two homosexuals up close and personal, which may never happen again in our lifetime. They shared their prospective—no, Dan shared his prospective with us, and we in turn shared the Word of God. At the end of the day, Dan and Cane were still two people who needed our help, and that, my daughter, is what being a Christian is all about—helping and being there for others."

"Dad, why is it that you can make sense out of everything?"

"I wouldn't go that far. Baby girl, I think I'm going to lie down now. Go back to bed and get a good night's sleep so we can begin this vacation."

"Dad, one more thing. Do you think God was testing us?"

"Absolutely. Remember, it's ten percent action, and ninety percent reaction."

"Is this one of those unexpected powerhouse blows?"

"Yes, indeed. Thanks for the reminder."

"Good night again, and love you, Dad."

"Love you too, baby girl."

Sarah hesitantly returned to the room, and before entering, she turned and blew her father a kiss. He smiled.

An "unexpected powerhouse blow" was a term used by Helen when Sarah had a personal challenge. A family of three moved into the neighborhood with their daughter named Abigail. She was the same age as Sarah, and they quickly became best friends. Helen immediately noticed troubling characteristics and cautiously monitored their association—a mother's intuition. They were teens and often were always finding themselves and behaving oddly.

There were cheerleader tryouts for middle school, and both girls wanted to become cheerleaders. Sarah was dedicated, practicing often, and she had taken courses. Their scheduled tryout time was seven in the morning, and due to an overwhelming response, the judges were strict with the crowded schedule—be on time, no exception.

One particular morning, Helen had committed to assist an elderly church member to an early medical appointment, and she had to leave around six forty-five. Prior to leaving, Helen asked Sarah if she wanted to be dropped off at Abigail's, and she confidently said no. Helen thought it peculiar for Abigail to suggest she come by and get Sarah. Her home was not only on the way to school but closer. She chalked it up to kids being odd.

Five minutes to seven, seven, and then ten minutes later, there was no Abigail. Sarah was beyond frantic and ran all the way to Abigail's home. Her mother answered the door and said Abigail had left long ago to be on time for tryouts. To make matters worse, her mom said Abigail told her Sarah was meeting her at the school. She started to cry and ran all the way to the gymnasium and arrived at seven twenty-five. She was too late and missed the tryouts. Sarah desperately attempted to speak to the judges, but to no avail. She went outside alone and began to cry profusely.

The bell rang for first period, and she walked sluggishly and depressed toward class. Sarah noticed Abigail at her locker and furiously rushed to confront her. As she approached Abigail, she looked at Sarah with utter cockiness and asked what happened to her. Sarah screamed and reminded her that she had given her word to pick her up. She responded that Sarah was crazy, and anyone with common sense would have known better, and furthermore, she was running late and didn't have time to get her. Sarah was furious and called her a liar. Abigail pushed her to the floor and left, laughing. Other students started calling her names, and she was surrounded by laughing childish spectators. Sarah picked herself up, charged at Abigail, and a fight ensued.

Neither of the girls was suspended; however, both parents had to meet with the principal. Sarah was beyond distraught. She surrendered into dark silence and refused to leave her room for two days, and this meant not attending school. No one was able to reach her. She was shutting down. Helen thought it was a simple but unfortunate situation, but Sarah, on the other hand, felt her world had crumbled. Her parents were struggling with how to deal with Sarah's agony. Pastor Haugen pondered how members incessantly sought his counseling for their children, and now the table had turned.

On day three, as Helen awoke, her spirit of helplessness spun into a protective uncompromising mother. She said to her husband, "Anders, the devil is a liar, and he shall not have our daughter. Not this day or any other day." She went to Sarah's room, tapped on the door, and walked in.

"Sarah. Sarah. Honey, get up. We need to talk."

She walked over to the blinds and opened them.

"Mom, what are you doing? Please close them."

"Not this day, sweetheart. Get up! We need to talk."

Sarah sat up.

"Mom, what's wrong?"

"You are what's wrong. Your father and I are deeply hurt with what happened between you and Abigail. It was mean-spirited, and I know you truly like her as a friend. Guess what, Sarah? Yes, you were lied to. You trusted someone who let you down and missed an opportunity to do something you really wanted to do and, furthermore, prepared for. Sorry to tell you this, but this has happened to me so many times in my life that I've lost count. Our fallen world is full of people who lie without blinking and do terrible things without giving it a second thought. Oh, and one more thing, Christians included. Thank God in heaven you have your family who loves and supports you. You have the Holy Spirit, the blood of Jesus, and your angel, or angels, whose divine duty is to watch over you. Get up, dust yourself off, and prove to the world you are more than a conqueror. Hold your beautiful head up and watch what God will do. Let's call what happened to you an "unexpected powerhouse blow." You got a knockdown, sweetheart, and there will be more to come. I can promise you that as your mother."

"Mom, she really hurt me."

"I know, sweetheart. Don't let shame rule you right now. In a few days, things will return to normal, and the drama will be with someone else. Right?"

"Right! Thank you, Mom."

"No, don't thank me. Thank God alone. Stop crying. Joy is here in the morning. Look at the sun coming through your window. Shower, get cute, eat breakfast, and go to school. Hold your head up. Hold it up so high that you almost trip on yourself."

They share a laugh as Helen embraced Sarah, and before she opened the door to leave, she said, "By the way, Abigail isn't your friend, and she is no longer welcome in our home. If she speaks, fine. If not, that's okay too. You got that."

"Yeah, Mom."

After that experience with Abigail, Sarah became the wiser and made it for cheerleader the following year, only to discover she'd rather compete in swimming.

As Pastor Haugen finally decided to return to the big bear recliner in hopes of getting a few hours of sleep, Dan opened the door. He headed back to the table, and Dan joined him.

"May I?"

Pastor Haugen extended his hands.

"So, you are having difficulty sleeping as well."

"Oh, yes. I'm not the healthiest person, and I need to take some meds to take the edge off."

"Do you need water?"

"That would be nice. Thank you."

He gets a glass from the cabinet.

"Tap or cold?"

"Tap. Thank you."

Dan discreetly took his cannabis pill and drank the water.

"Pastor Haugen, I did not come out here to go another round with you. Once is enough."

"I have no intentions on arguing. I've said what I needed to say to the both of you. However, just out of sheer curiosity, if you were raised a Catholic, how did you end up an atheist out of all things?"

"You said you were done."

"Forgive me for not being totally truthful."

"I've never been able to comprehend how devoted people of God sometimes unfailingly continuously get the raw end of the stick when, in fact, they should be blessed beyond measure."

"Who do or did you know get the raw end of the stick? Was it you?"

"No, and why would you ask if it were someone I knew?"

"Most atheist were previously Christians. Were you sorely hurt by some woman?"

"Are you attempting to do a table talk redemption?"

"Not at all. You're too intelligent for that type of psychology."

"So now you believe hurt is the driving force for an atheist to make intelligent, informed decisions.

"Need I say to a previous Christian that God allows the rain to fall on the just and the unjust. As human beings, we are absolutely spoiled and expect God to say yes to each and every time we go to him, but it's rather unrealistic. And when God says no or something doesn't happen the way we anticipate, we get disrespectfully angry. After all, we deserve everything we ask, right?"

"Pastor Haugen, doesn't your scripture say, ask and it shall be given to you? Is that a contradiction or a post-blessing abstract?"

"Now who's playing a psychological tenet here? That scripture is pertaining to anyone seeking the Holy Spirit and not to be twisted as the prosperity pulpits have eloquently goaded down the sanctuary aisles and in the minds of people not fully understanding the Word."

"Bravo, Pastor!" he said as he softly and pretentiously clapped.

"So poor soulless individuals as myself chose any miniscule excuse not to believe in God, and defiled pulpits are just casualties of spiritual war."

"I never in my life heard it put that way, but close."

"Since we're divulging gnostic anomalies. It wasn't, by no means, an easy process, but a prompt deliverance from wasting my time. I believe in my own efforts to obtain whatever it is I need or want to achieve."

Pastor Haugen was silent.

"As you said, an intelligent, informed decision."

"Sexual orientation included."

"No one can say you don't have all the bases covered."

"You loathe my lifestyle, and I expect it from you and your kind. Does the term 'your kind' make you feel uncomfortable?"

"On the contrary, peculiarity is one of many characteristics I possess while holding up the bloodstain banner of my Lord and Savior Jesus Christ."

Pastor Haugen and Dan's indulgence of borderline contempt had tipped another boiling point, howbeit, as calm and unyielding their postures.

"You may loathe my lifestyle, but others may say, 'Yes, God loves everyone.'"

"Oh, you're slipping now, Dan."

"Really? How so?"

"Oh, yeah. You should know out of all people that lie is orchestrated by the master of illusionist, Satan. If everyone believes God loves everyone and accepts everything, all of our behaviors—good, bad, or unnatural—are acceptable, which makes the Word null and void, the antithesis of His nature, the lie of lies, God accepts everything."

Dan whispered, "You should be having this conversation with Cane."

"If you need more water, help yourself," Pastor Haugen said as he excused himself and went to the big bear.

Deep inside, Pastor Haugen was disappointed with Cane and empathized for his father who was also a pastor.

Dan was not feeling well, and the incidents of the day had weakened him to the point of thinking, perhaps, South Lake Tahoe should have been postponed as he initially considered.

THE DARKNESS OF DAWN

Pastor Haugen had slept only a few hours, and now he had made a decision that was best for the entire household. Looking at the large clock in the living room, it was seven minutes after five. He went to the closet, got his coat, slipped on his shoes, and took a set of keys out of the utility box on the coatroom shelf. Heading out the back door toward the garage, he picked up a flashlight near the floor. The snow offered shadowed light, and it is bone cold.

In the garage was a green 2009 Toyota Tacoma. Pastor Haugen always believed when vacationing to keep an additional vehicle nearby. The kids used it mostly in the summer when weather conditions were more favorable. He started the truck, and it was half-full. Now the contemplating was whether to proceed with his plans while the truck is warming or not.

"I've got to do this," he said.

He opened the garage and sat in the warm truck for more than ten minutes. It ran perfectly.

He slowly drove the truck on the side of the house and said, "Lord, give me strength."

There was dead silence in the air, and you can hear the wind blowing off your ear. Returning to the house, he tapped Cane on his feet.

"Cane. Cane."

"Yes, Pastor, is something wrong?"

"No, I would like for you and Dan to use my truck and leave now before anyone gets up. Not the Escalade, I have a Tacoma outside we keep in the garage. Sorry to have to do this, but it's best. Would you please wake Dan up and let him know?"

"Sure, no problem."

Cane lethargically went into Dan's room and returned alone a few minutes later.

"He's getting his things together."

"Thank you. I know this is an inconvenience, but it's best. You can keep the truck until your road service arrives. Remember the intersection about five miles back with a restaurant and auto shop, Joe's?"

"Not really."

"Anyway, it's Joe's. As another favor, please take the truck and leave it there, not here. He'll recognize the truck, and we've known him for years. It'll be fine."

"In other words, stay the heck away?"

Pastor Haugen did not respond. Instead, he returned to the kitchen and prepared a pot of coffee. TJ scratched the door and began to whine. He hurried to keep anyone from hearing.

"Shhh!" he said as he led him out the back door.

Cane sat on the edge of the sofa, assembling his footwear, and then fumbled in his duffel bag.

"Are you okay over there?"

Cane turned and looked at him scornfully, not uttering one sound. Pastor Haugen was feeling the guilt of waking them with such a sudden request and was tempted to offer coffee. He walked over to Cane and patted him on the back.

"Son, you are, perhaps, a lot more angry with yourself than me. I'm not about to say anything to you that I'm certain your father, a pastor, hasn't already said. I just want to leave you with this. Jesus said the truth shall set you free. Freedom not from shackles." Pastor Haugen held his wrist in making a point. "Freedom is here in the mind where it starts and ends. You've been quite silent since Dan made that statement last night. There's a time to speak and a time to be silent. You care to share anything with me while it's just you and I?"

Cane continued to fumble with his bag and said nothing.

Pastor Haugen sighed. TJ was pawing at the door, and he went to let him in. Upon his return, Dan emerged.

"Good morning, Dan. I think it's best the both of you leave now to avoid any awkwardness."

"Not a problem, Pastor Haugen. Thanks for everything. Just think you could have asked us to leave last night, but this way is much more dignified. Just kidding. Please thank your lovely family for being so gracious as well."

"I've given Cane instructions regarding the truck, and, Cane, the keys are in the truck. I'll be praying for the both of you. I will."

"I'll get your bag—you look awful," said Cane.

"And good morning to you too. I look better than I feel." He gave Pastor Haugen a half salute and left. Pastor Haugen returned the quirky salute.

Cane lifted the black duffel bag and walked to the door with his head bowed in utter degradation. Reaching to push the screen, he stopped momentarily and, in a stare down to Pastor Haugen, defiantly said, "Pastor Haugen, before a person can make an exodus, you must first have entered. You remember this! Before a person can make an exodus, he must first have entered."

He stoically received the mysterious parting statement. Relieved to finally have the guests out of his home, he leaned back against the closed door exhausted.

"Father God, please be with those two. What was that all about? I'm glad this is over!"

Cane headed to the parked truck, and Dan was standing inside the passenger door, watching him. As he approached the truck, he was shaking his head, and his facial expression exuded irritation.

"Cane, are you okay?" asked Dan.

He opened the door and, with a detestable stare, said, "Please don't say anything to me. I don't want to talk about this."

"I'm just asking if you are okay."

"Okay? Are you kidding me? Are you fricking kidding me? What do you know about being okay? You ruined everything. Everything was going just fine until you just had to take it upon yourself and say, 'Oh, yes, by the way, we are gay'!"

"What is your problem? You really need to chill out."

"Wow! Chill out, you say! And you didn't even have the decency to discuss with me first sharing my personal business with this family. You had no right at all."

"Decency to discuss! Now you are kidding me. Why not? Well, we are! What was wrong with me telling them? What is really wrong with you?"

"I don't want to talk about this. Let's just get away from here—the sooner the better!"

"I don't get you! You have some nerve. I only supposed you wanted them to know, especially since you were so freely sharing your life story."

"Dan, you are such a pathetic liar."

"Cane, do not call me a liar again!"

"Oh, spare me. You are a liar!"

"I'm warning you, Cane!"

"Or what?"

Cane struck his chest, saying, "I was enjoying myself being around people who genuinely had something in common with me. In common with me. That was the problem, and you couldn't handle it. Let's face it. You were jealous!"

"Jealous! Now I know you've gone over the edge here."

"What else would compel you to divulge my private business to strangers? Admit it! I was in my element, not yours, and you couldn't stand it."

"Element! Wow! So Christians are your element, and my social circle is what? Tell me."

"Why waste my time dignifying this foolishness!"

"Wow. You are certainly full of surprises, Cane. As I recall, even among my intimate friends, you've never once openly admitted you were gay or expressed any of our values. With me and my friends, you have this façade of being an extremely private person. Oh, but with the Hagenses, you tell your life's history."

"Didn't you hear me? I said I don't want to discuss this."

"Uh-uh! No! Let's get this out now! I've never seen you laugh as much as you did here. Never, Cane. Now what's wrong with this picture? And around this family you acted as though you loath me. One would suspect you have some sort of mental disorder."

"Who I am and how I relate to anyone is none of your damn business!"

"Oh, I know who you are, trust me! And don't think for a moment I didn't hear what you said to the pastor before we left. What's up with that? Now you're full of riddles. Be a man and stop behaving like some wounded spoiled little boy. Be a man and stand up for who you are!"

"Well, well, well! Little boy! Be a man! Spoiled! Dan, would you say it's better than being a pathetic, lonely, and miserable philanthropist? Oh, and did I mention your time is almost up anyway?"

Cane smirked, placed the bag in the rear seat, and started the truck. Dan was emotionally devastated and got in the car, looking straight down ahead the steep drive. In a subdued tone, he said, "How dare you speak to me in this manner, you smug, pompous, pretentious piece of work! From the night in Sausalito until now, I have provided you with a comfortable place to live so you could get yourself together. Not to mention I pay you generously, I might add, in order to give you a sense of dignity. Dignity! All I asked of you was to assist me during this difficult time in my life. That was all! Nothing more! You want to know why I did all of these things?"

"Shut up and leave me alone. Is that all you can pull out of your bag of tricks? Trust me, I've been called worst. You're pathetic. Shut the hell up, I said."

"I did all of this because I thought I saw myself in you as a young man, and I wanted to help you. Did you hear me? Help you! How outright imprudent of me! And to think the entire time we were here you pretended to be something you aren't. One thing is for sure, I know who I am! Did you hear me? I know who I am!" Dan screamed and, with a maddening force, banged the dashboard with his right hand as he stared at Cane.

In a composed voice, he responded, "No! Dan, you have this all wrong. You are clueless as to who I am. All wrong. Everything was fine! In your little twisted world, you needed once again in your life to feel rejection so you, my friend, can be justified in who you really are. You've been rejected so long that it comes naturally to self-sabotage. I may be young and have my issues, but I know something about people. Let's see what the psychological term here is. Yes, you wanted me to feel that natural progression of rejection like you!"

"Rejected!"

In a feminine tone, Cane taunted Dan.

"Oh, well, let me tell them I'm gay. Here it comes! Natural rejection! Pain needs passengers, so take Cane. Why should he be happy if I'm not? Boohoo!"

Cane reverted to his normal voice. "Your recipe! A comfortable place to stay, yes! Generous, yes! And with a large portion of insecurity and a dash of vindictiveness, and what do you get? You get Mr. Daniel Piattoni, the benevolent atheist on his way to hell in a handbasket."

"You really don't know who I am, do you? Insulting me will not change this reality. You are not like them and probably never will be. Yes, I told them we were gay. Certainly! And maybe I should have been quiet about it. So what? I admit I felt slighted with how you were treating me, and I needed to pull your cocky coattail."

Cane repulsively looked at Dan. "Oh my God, I knew it!"

"Let's face facts here. You needed a dose of reality."

"What did you say?"

"Look how the Haugens treated you when they learned the truth! And you say I'm pathetic and on my way to hell. It's none of my business, but I question if you really are gay and frankly I couldn't care less. The truth of the matter is it's all on you. All on you, buddy!"

"You're right. It's none of your business. Now since we've moved on to telling the truth, I despise you! Literally! Yes, I honestly despise you. How liberating. I said it. You disgust me!"

Dan blew an exhaustive whistle.

"Well, at least, you are man enough to finally say it. So you hate me. Now what? Cane, I do know who I am, and another thing is for certain, I know my patience has worn out, and I'm tired. It's been my observation in all sincerity that you, my young friend, don't know who or what you really are, or what you want to be. And sadly, you are alone with your tormentors and appear to have no one. Your make-believe family session we just encountered proves even more that you are delusional. Oh, yes, delusional. How troubling! When we return to the city, please make immediate arrangements to leave my home. The sooner, the better! I strongly recommend you go back to Kentucky and salvage what's left of your tumultuous life."

Silence blew in Cane's ear as snow crushed under the tires of a slow-moving vehicle in the distance. Silence.

"Throughout my entire life, I heard my father say over and over that it's not what goes into a man that defiles his body, but what comes out the mouth. Inside, you are nothing but dried-up rotten stinking bones. A man who turned his back on God and now calls himself an atheist. Sad!" And he ostentatiously laughed.

"Really? Well, would your father say a man is gay if he slept with a man once? I'm of the opinion that, yes, especially, if they can't hold their liquor. What do you suppose? My dear Jeffrey Cane

Peters, yes, your real name. And for the record, what I heard last night about your family is old news. I've known all about you from day one. Not the few details you provided last night, but enough. Do you really think I would allow a psychopath to live with me? I think not. Now drive, please."

Cane's mouth began to quiver. His eyes were swollen, and a tear rolled past his nose, over his mouth, and onto his lap. He released the brake and drove the truck slowly down the black-tarred drive onto the road.

Was Cane distraught for fear of being homeless or leveled with the veracity of his life? In that instance, he realized Dan had gone beyond a slight interest into his past, and more of an intrusive nature. How long had he known? Why didn't he say anything before now? Cane felt grossly deceived.

The two fatigued houseguests had managed to give way to raw bitterness toward one another with the determination to dehumanize. True vulnerability revealed both yearned-for inclusiveness and, more importantly, acceptance.

Meanwhile, back at Blue Castle...

Pastor Haugen was sitting at the large empty table and let out a large sigh. Helen appeared.

"Anders! You okay?"

"Who knows? How in God's name did our lives get turned upside down in, what, seven hours or so?"

Helen nodded.

"I can tell you haven't slept. Did you sleep at all?"

"Not really. I dozed off and on in the big brown bear. I let them borrow the truck until they get their business squared away. I asked them to return it to Joe's and not bother returning it here."

"Honey, you didn't say it like that, did you?"

"No, no. Thank God we have the Tacoma, and to think I was going to sell it last year. Yikes. I'll call the shop when it opens and ask Joe to notify us when they drop it off."

"That was good thinking on your part!"

"I got up a little while ago and politely asked them to leave before anyone was awake. I wanted to prevent an awkward morning and not take a chance on any type of confrontation. Honey, when the kids get up, I'll tell them they got up early, and I decided to loan them the truck. Nothing, please, about me asking them to leave. It's not a lie, and it's not the entire truth either, but it's best. God help me."

"You did the right thing, Anders, and God knows your heart and intent. I believe I heard them arguing. At first, I thought I was dreaming, but when I got up to see what was going on, they had already driven off. Were they arguing?"

"Yeah, I heard bits and pieces and purposely drowned it out. With those two…that's on them, and there's no telling what they were going at it about!"

"Can you believe Cane's father is a pastor, and he decides to be gay? Oh my Lord, Cane's parents are surely heartbroken. Babe, we would not have suspected a thing until Dan told us. Why do you think he did that? Do you believe he wanted to see if we approved of their lifestyle?"

"I don't know. I've asked myself the same question. Why even tell us? Was it just me? But did you pick up Cane's annoyance with Dan when he said they were gay?"

"Oh, yeah. Anders, I don't believe he wanted us to know."

"Do you blame him? It seemed that way."

"The way Cane shared his life story with us, he had a decent Christian home upbringing. How did he, out of all people, end up attracted to other men? Cane seemed so normal. You know what I'm trying to say."

In a low-fatigued voice, he replied, "I know. No need to explain." He could barely keep his eyes open as he laid his head over his arms at the table.

"While it's on my mind, don't you dare beat yourself up about inviting those two in here. I know you, Anders. Don't! Oh, I'm serious. Regardless of what happened here last night, you helped two people in need and extended genuine kindness toward strangers. Yes, any decent person would have followed in your footsteps."

"Helen, it's over now, thank God. Let me get some rest and hit the reset button on this vacation when I wake up."

"You're right, Anders. But one last thing, and then I will say no more. Last night, remember when I hugged Cane? It was as if he hung on to me for dear life. It's obvious he misses his family. Nine times out of ten they alienated him. Maybe through us, God wanted Cane to see what he left behind in hopes of leaving that sinful lifestyle. And there could have been a message for Dan, once a Christian and now an atheist. I don't get it. Only a foolish man lives apart from God like that. I'm sorry, honey. I'll be quiet. You can hardly keep your eyes open. Time for you to begin this vacation. Go to bed. I'll call the shop and ask the kids to keep it down until you get some rest."

"While this is on my mind, I've decided we are going to have an open family discussion about last night. To be more candid, we need to be prepared if one or all three throw us a curve. I'm convinced last night was a wake-up call for this family, and it is imperative we're on the same page. By all accounts, we did the right thing by helping strangers in need, but a line has to be drawn in the sand. Our kids need to remember to be on the side of the Lord regardless of peer pressure or whatever else confronts them."

"That's an excellent idea. And please don't beat yourself up because of Cane's personal decision."

"Helen, it's difficult not to think about them."

"Honey, I know. You're tired, and we have the rest of the week to discuss this."

Pastor Haugen could barely stand straight. He hugged Helen and left for the bedroom occupied by Dan. Suddenly, she rushed behind him.

"No, don't go to bed yet. Let me change the linen. It'll only take a minute."

"Please, Helen. It's no big deal."

"Yes, it is. Not on my watch."

He sat in the chair next to the dresser, forcing his eyes to remain open. Helen quickly took the yellow set of linen from the hall closet and moved as though she was in a race for time, tucking and pulling effortlessly.

"Done. Babe, come on." She fluffed the two queen-size pillows.

She took his left arm and guided him to the bed, removing his green fleece shirt as he kicked off his loafers.

"Thanks, Helen. What time is it?"

"Why are you concerned about the time? You aren't going anywhere."

"I don't know why I asked that silly question."

Leaving the room, she whispered, "Go to sleep. If you must know, it's about five forty-five."

Helen went to the window next to the door, taking a glimpse of the snow that lit the dawning sky. Then reverently, she knelt down and began to passionately pray. The strangers were gone, and the indelible scene lingered like fading smoke in the wind. Her spirit was not fearful, only concerned, about what happened earlier, and she desired more protection from God. She was spiritually discerned, realizing our world coexisted with an unseen world and that her family was now exposed. Unclean spirits had entered her home. Her prayer was for God to release His power and remove any unclean and illegal spirits. Demonic spirits are stubborn, and if not called out correctly, they resist leaving, so their acts must be identified when praying. God's spiritual authority has dominion over any demonic being—any!

Unclean spirits didn't literally mean dirty, but a demonic spirit enslaving the body who was accusing and opposing the will of God. Heavenly and demonic spirits are warring continuously. In the unseen world, there is authority, order beyond our human comprehension, and dominion on both sides. Just as generation after generation had not seen our Lord and Savior, they did, however, witness His foundations of faith lain spirit by spirit. Believing in our Lord, you also believe in the real and ever-present enemy of God: the old serpent, the accuser—Satan.

> When the unclean spirit is gone out of a man, he walketh throughout dry places, seeking rest, and findeth none. Then he saith, I will return into my house from whence I came out; and when he is come, he findeth it empty, swept, and garnished. Then goeth he, and taketh with himself seven other spirits more wicked than himself, and they enter in and dwell there: and the last state of that man is worse than the first. Even so shall it be also unto this wicked generation. (Matt. 12:43–45)

Helen was a faithful believer in the infinite power of prayer, and when a deeper meditation was warranted, she burned frankincense or did sage smudging.

The burning of incense dates back as far as human history is recorded. The mesmerizing aroma heightens the senses during prayer and ceremonial acts. It is believed to purify the area and create a calm mood beneficial to true meditation of hearing and speaking to God. Centuries ago, a purer form of frankincense was used, and it was expensive. Frankincense was one of the three gifts mentioned in biblical history the holy family received from one of the kings when our Lord and Savior was very young. More than likely, it was used for their offering and times of prayer—a divine symbolism worthy of following today.

Helen had frankincense resins she kept at home and at the Blue Castle. She sat by the fireplace and lit her frankincense, closed her eyes, and began to breathe consciously—breathing in, breathing out.

"Oh, Heavenly Father, thank you, thank you, thank you."

Silence.

"Father God, I need you. The two strangers we allowed in our home had unclean sexual spirits. I ask that you cleanse our home and remove any and all evil spirits that have entered and are dwelling."

Silence.

"Protect us and bless our dwelling place. Thank you."

Silence.

"Father, be with Dan and Cane. Their souls are in jeopardy."

Silence.

"Please continue to guide us into your holy truths and not our own thinking in this fallen world."

Silence.

"Gird Anders with physical strength and wisdom as he guides this family."

Silence.

"Please pour your healing and cleansing power over Blue Castle. I love you. I love you. I love you. Thank you.

Silence.

"I offer up these prayers, and I ask that it be your will."

Silence.

"Yes. Yes."

Silence.

"The alpha. The omega. And your name, every knee shall bow. Every knee. It is in your name, Jesus, I pray. Amen"

Helen's meditative praying lasted forty-five minutes. Arising, her heart was lightened as she felt the Holy Spirit come over her; the intimate prayers were heard. She placed another log in the fire and continued to enjoy her tranquil space.

THE GONE FACTOR

9:30 a.m.

"Morning, Mom! Where is everyone?" Sarah asked.

"Morning!"

"Where's everyone? Did Mr. Dan and Cane leave?"

"Yes, they left earlier, and your dad is in the room sleeping, so we all need to hold it down."

"I didn't mean to sleep so late. Andrew and Pete still sleeping? TJ! TJ!" Sarah sang.

"Shhh! Let him out. I believe I heard your brothers a minute ago. They should be out soon."

"I'll get breakfast started. Go see if they are up and tell them to keep it down and that our guests are gone."

All the kids appeared from the room and were enthusiastically anticipating the day. They'd decided to go skiing about five miles north at one of their favorite resorts. The vote was cast, and omelets were the item of the morning. As the conversations ensued surrounding the previous night, Helen maneuvered with mild avoidance to keep the momentum going in another direction.

12:15 p.m.

Pastor Haugen had rested, and Helen was preparing a late break-fast for her husband. The kids were gathering their packs. It was clear and snow-packed, and the weather was perfect. Helen had decided to remain in and continue her reading, while Pastor Haugen would do a little tinkering in the garage. His cell phone rang.

"Will one of you please get that for me?"

"I got it," said Andrew as he ran to get it.

Andrew noticed it was the church.

"It's the church, Dad."

"Oh my, let me see what's going on."

He got up from the table and walked over to the bay window.

"Hello. Hi, Dora. Fine. Everyone's enjoying the vacation. Sure, no problem. You did the right thing. Thank you. I appreciate it. Lord willing, I'll see you soon too! Good-bye and thanks again."

"Honey, what's going on?"

"A friend of Dan's…" His cell phone rang again.

"Hold on, honey. Hello. This is Pastor Haugen. Yes, Yes. Uh-huh. What? When? How are they doing? What? Oh my God! No! No! Sure, I know where it is. Just a moment, I need something to write with. Room 721. Got it. So sorry, what is your name again? Nathaniel Horowitz. Horowitz. Give me about an hour or sooner. Not a problem. Good-bye."

Helen handed him a pen and paper as he wrote down the details. She and the kids gathered round to hear what had him upset. Pastor Haugen turned off the phone and asked everyone to have a seat.

"What happened, Anders?"

"It's bad."

"What is it?" Helen asked.

"Dan and Cane were in an accident in the Tacoma when they left here this morning."

"How are they doing?" asked Helen.

"Cane is dead!

"What? Oh, no, no, Anders." Helen cried.

"Dad, he's dead?" asked Andrew.

"Yes, Dan is in critical condition at the hospital and is not expected to pull through. That was his attorney, and Dan requested to see me."

"Oh, Dad," Sarah said as she hugged her dad.

Helen went to the bedroom and closed the door. She remembered hugging Cane last night, and she couldn't help but think he may have sensed it was his last time seeing her. The Haugens were now mourning strangers whom they'd known less than twenty-four hours and affected their lives profoundly. Pastor Haugen sat on the edge of the big bear, stunned, and the kids occupied the sofa.

"The hospital contacted Mr. Horowitz, his attorney. He flew here with others on a private jet. Dan requested he contact me, so Mr. Horowitz contacted the church. Dear God. Unbelievable! Poor Cane. I just spoke to him a few hours ago, giving him some fatherly advice, and now he's gone. Gone."

"Dad, was another car involved? How did it happen?" asked Peter.

"I don't know. I didn't ask for the details."

"This entire vacation is something out of a horror movie. Insane! Cane is dead. Wow!" added Andrew.

Sarah sat on the sofa and cried.

"Anyone care to go with me? I'm taking TJ for a walk. I need some air. Unbelievable," Peter said.

"I need to shower and get up to the hospital. Kids pray for this entire situation. People are hurting," Pastor Haugen said as he went into the bedroom.

"Helen, how are you doing?"

"Anders, this is so heartbreaking. Who was that on the phone?"

"Dan's attorney. He and a few others flew up here on a private plane."

"I can't get over yesterday. We had dinner, laughing, and then the evening went south, they left early this morning, and now Cane is dead, and Dan's hanging on to dear life. This is so much to take in one day. Too much. Anders, I prayed earnestly this morning for the both of them. Earnestly, and now this."

"Honey, listen to yourself. Please don't do this and don't lose sight. Your prayers were heard. Dan could have died along with Cane, but God is granting him time. Time for what, I don't know."

"Lose sight? Why did you even stop?"

"What?"

"Maybe something else should have been done. Drove them home or something."

"You agreed, even insisted, we invite them in."

"You didn't have to listen to me."

"I'm going to ignore that last statement. You're tired and need to get some rest."

"Please don't patronize me. Not now."

"Patronize you. What are you talking about?"

"We work our butts off all through the year doing this, doing that. We were close to being burned out, especially this year. Burned completely out! Still smiling, but completely burned-out. Blue Castle is the one place we decompress and breathe easier away from it all for a while."

"You don't think I'm exhausted, but I don't blame others for it."

"I didn't blame you, Anders."

"Helen, yes, in your own roundabout way, you did."

"No, I didn't. I just said maybe something else should have been done when we first met them, like unpack and drive them home."

"Helen, why are you nitpicking? It's over. What's done is done. Now you're trying to make me feel guilty for a decision I made. I did what I thought was best. Thanks a lot. Jeez! I need to shower and get to the hospital."

"I'm not blaming you. It's just a bad set of circumstances spiraling who knows where. We are only human. It's too much. Too much!"

He walked toward the bathroom and turned around.

"Sarah woke up last night, and we chatted briefly. Do you know what our daughter reminded me of? An unexpected power-house blow."

Helen mused.

"This one came swift, hard, and, yes, we are getting slammed. It's part of who we are and what we are committed to do as Christians. We were used to having our cushiony getaway. Look around you, Helen—snowcapped mountains and million-dollar views. And guess what? We are continuing our tradition. Nothing's really changed except our attitude."

He looked, awaiting a response, and the moment he turned to go to shower, she thoughtfully spoke.

"You're right. Anders, I'm overwhelmed, that's all. Do you suppose Dan has decided to confess Jesus Christ is Lord before he dies?"

"Could be. It's been known to happen."

"Then by all means, go see him before it's too late. And you be careful and take your sweet time. Cane may have repented himself. You never know."

Helen's facial expression was now that of trepidation.

"Oh, no!"

"What is it?"

"Anders, his parents are going to be shattered."

He anchored out a large sigh.

"Helen, hold it together, please. We've got to pray for everyone."

She sat on the bed, took a tissue from the nightstand, and wiped her eyes.

"The kids are having a rough time too. Talk to them. They need the both of us to hold it together."

"I will. I heard Peter say he was going for a walk. Maybe I will join them. Fresh air would be good right about now."

"What hospital is he in?"

"Kaiser. I need to hurry up and shower."

"We'll wait until you leave before we go."

"No need."

"Yes, Anders, I insist."

"I'm not in an arguing mood."

"I'll ask the kids to hold tight until you leave. Maybe hang around the front or something."

Pastor Haugen was dressed and preparing to leave. The family was somberly sitting around the front porch.

"Do you have everything? Your phone?"

"I've got my phone, and it's charged up. Let's offer up a prayer. Come closer, kids. Hold hands."

"Heavenly Father, we are so thankful once again for another blessed day to give praise and honor to your holy and righteous name. Our hearts are heavy now. We are mourning the loss of our guest, Cane. Be with his family and friends. Please comfort them during this time." He was silent.

"Father God, we are asking that you be with Dan this hour. May the medical staff comfort him and have a sound knowledge of treatment to administer to him during this time. Have mercy on his soul, and I pray all pride and issues of life be removed from his spirit so that he may call your name before it is everlasting too late. Be with his dear friends as they begin the grieving process. Comfort them, please. Continue to be with me as the father over our home that I may always seek you for wisdom and comfort, and please let me be a source of strength and encouragement. I ask that you comfort my entire family during this time. We so love and need you. Father God, please watch over all of us as we now go our separate ways. It is in your Son Jesus's name I pray, let us all say, Amen."

"Amen."

Helen and the Haugenbunch watched him leave into the distant as they headed off for the snow.

EYES OF RECOMPENSE

Pastor Haugen walked down the hospital corridor, looking at all the faces and, within seconds, reading their pain and imagining the cause—an odd habit practiced his entire life. As he stepped into the elevator, an anxious little boy stood with his father. As he reached to push button 7, the anxious boy asked, "What floor?"

"Seven. Thank you."

"I have a new little brother. His name is Stephen. My dad said I can call him Steve."

"That's enough, son! He's excited about having our new addition to the family. We're on our way to bring my wife and the baby home," the proud father explained.

"Congratulations! No need to explain. I have three, and I felt the same about each one of them."

"Thank you, sir. Here's our floor. Son, tell the nice man good-bye."

"Bye. My mommy and Steve are leaving today! They are coming home."

Pastor Haugen stepped aside, waving at the little boy. "God bless you."

The door closed, and he thought to himself how innocent life is at that age, as it should.

A soft buzz and the elevator door opened to the seventh floor. Room 721 was in the west wing. Turning the corner, everyone was attentive to their task at the nurse's station, and his presence was hardly unnoticed. One nurse smiled at him, and he returned with a cordial nod.

"It's 717, 719 and 721," he mumbled to himself.

Standing in front of room 721, he paused for a few seconds, as if to listen, and abruptly stepped back. In a cowardly fit, he turned and headed back toward the elevator. Looking suspicious as though someone knew he abandoned his appointment, he dashed into an empty elevator and insanely continuously pushed the lobby button.

"I don't know this man. What difference does it make if I don't show up? I don't owe him anything. Why did I ask them into my home? Nothing but trouble, and all of this on my watch! God, I should have never stopped. Never!" he said, followed by a loud horrible sigh.

As the door opened, an East Indian family of four graciously stepped aside for his exit. An aged couple held hands, while the female appeared to lean more on her husband for physical support. Two middle-aged men, who bore a strong resemblance of the couple, were probably their sons. All were wearing expressions of anguish, as if the voice of death blew a faint whisper in their ears. Their eyes sorrowfully followed him as though he had some bestowed words of comfort to say.

Strolling out of the building with his head bowed, he avoided any eye contact. The cold fresh Tahoe air helped him breathe again. Small snow flurries sprinkled the view as he inhaled for inner peace. He adjusted his coat collar and asked God what His profound purpose was in all this chaos and tragedy. The Prophet Jonah immediately enveloped his mind. He knew then it was not right to leave, but he was not ready to face the atheist stranger or the attorney who phoned either. Over his left shoulder was the window of the vacant waiting room. He decided to take advantage of the peace and think about what to do next. His heart was grieving for the brief young soul whose last words to him were filled with sarcasm and disdain.

"God, perhaps, a great portion of my sorrow is clear mistake in judgment. All I can think of are three acts of kindness—offering my home to wait, a place for the night, and use of the truck. Father, you must know in my heart I was trying to do what I felt was right. One was killed, and the other probably on his way. Lord, have mercy!"

He began doubting all his actions up to checking the car before the trip and questioning if any mechanical problems would have happened had he driven it.

"Why should I subject myself to any further contact? We all said some things that were pretty darn mean to each other, but I am not going to back down from this gay stuff. It doesn't change the truth. It's just wrong, and they know it. The sheer arrogance of Cane! Pushing and pushing even right before he walked out the door. He was determined to make me angry and forced me to see life through his eyes. I had enough and just wanted them to get as far away from us as possible. All of this is my fault. Oh, Lord, what do I do now?"

"Pray. Just pray about it," said an unknown female voice.

He looked up, and a young pregnant woman was sitting behind him.

"Sir, I didn't mean to startle you, but you have been talking to yourself since I arrived. I did hear you clearly when you asked the Lord what to do. Don't mind me."

"How long have you been sitting there?"

"Maybe five minutes or so...long enough to know that your heart is heavy. I spoke to you when I sat down, but you didn't say anything. I just figured you weren't here."

"Jeez!"

"I take it you are a believer?"

"Yes!"

"Answers don't always come right away. Sometimes you have to just be still and let them gently fall on your heart."

"Thank you, young lady. When is your baby due?"

"In two months."

"Your first?"

"Well, the first this far. I lost two other babies. So far, so good, and I thank God."

"God bless you and this baby."

"Thank you, sir. My husband is in the army doing his third tour in Afghanistan."

"Oh, you must be proud."

"I am at that. I really miss him. We are Christians too, and he is such a good man. I'm here because of my grandpa. He's up in age and suffered a stroke, and he may leave us real soon if it's God's will."

"I'm so sorry!"

"Thank you, but please don't be sorry. He is eighty-eight years old and lived a good, good life. My grandma passed away three weeks ago, and she was eighty-five. She had been ill for some time. They were married sixty-six years. Can you believe that? We've barely had a chance to go through her things, and now this. It's been downhill for him ever since she crossed over. They were inseparable, and that's why I know she's waiting on him."

"I appreciate you sharing that with me. How beautiful. Married sixty-six years! You don't hear that often."

"Are your parents here?"

"No. My parents were killed in a two-car collision when I was eight, and my grandparents raised me. My mother was their only child. Grandpa is all I have here besides Marcus, my husband."

"You seemed to have had a bit of a rough road, haven't you? You didn't have to share all of this with me, but you did. I do appreciate it."

"It's true what they say. If you think your troubles are bad, just listen to someone else's. I will be all right. Quite a few of the church members are upstairs, and it's comforting to know my grandpa truly fought a good fight and kept the faith. I'm proof of that. Praise God. May I ask who you are visiting here, sir?"

"Can you believe this? A stranger! Someone I really don't know at all. He requested me. He was seriously injured in that accident on Junction 10 early this morning."

"Oh, I remember seeing something about that on the news. Didn't someone die?"

"Yes, there were two, and the one upstairs is the other one. I should not say I don't know them at all. As a matter of fact, I met them briefly."

"He's requesting you? Are you a pastor or spiritual person?"

"Yes, I am a pastor."

"Okay, that explains it."

"It is a little more complicated than that."

The female stranger stood, gathered her coat, and bottled water.

"Well, sir, I need to get back up to my grandpa. I only wanted to stretch my legs a spell, and to be honest, I don't know what convinced me to come down here. But I'm glad I decided to come."

"I would like to pray for you, if you don't mind?" he asked.

"Oh my goodness, yes!"

He stood, and they held hands.

"What is your name?"

"Samantha."

"I'm Pastor Anders Haugen."

"Nice to meet you, Pastor Haugen."

"Pleasure's been all mine, Samantha."

They bowed heads.

"Dear, Father God, thank you for allowing strangers' paths to cross. Please be with Samantha as she returns to her grandfather whom she loves so dearly. She stated he's been a faithful solider on the battlefield for years, and for this, we are both thankful. Give her peace and strength to endure any challenges ahead. Please provide her with all the necessary support during these difficult times. Continue to be with her during this pregnancy and protect her and the unborn baby. Bless this baby to enter this world healthy and free from any illness. Be with her husband, Marcus, and protect him so that he may return to her safe, without any harm or danger. Shower this family with your mercy and favor. This prayer I offer up to you. It is in Jesus's name, I pray. Amen."

"Pastor Haugen, thank you so much for praying for my family. I was supposed to be right here."

Samantha left, and he stepped over to the window again.

"Heavenly Father, I need you too. Please be with me. Amen."

Through the reflection of the window, he noticed people entering the room. It was as if for those few private minutes God had purposefully given them that little space and time. His emotions had been suspended in his mind too long, and it was now time to make the visit and the face the unknown.

Making his way back to the seventh floor, he knew some sort of closure was near, and this was an opportunity not for him, but for God. This time as he made his way toward room 721, two men and a female were standing in the hallway outside the room. Yes, they were here for Dan. The female, an attractive blonde in her late-thirties and sharply dressed in a black wool hat and coat, was crying uncontrollably. A tall man wearing a ski cap and jacket with dark shades was leaning against the wall. The older bald gentleman was embracing the woman and began to gently stroke her head.

"Good evening."

"Good evening!" said one of the men tearfully.

He began to contemplate if he had spent too much time chatting with the young lady and missed his meeting with Dan.

Gently knocking twice, he entered. Classical violin music was playing softly from an iPod, and a large bouquet of exotic beautiful flowers shared the tiny sterile hospital table. The room was dim, and Dan appeared to be hanging on to life. His face was mutilated with cuts almost to the point of visible unbearableness. His head, the left side of his face, and arms were wrapped in bandages. He had dark purple bruising down his nose. The IV was positioned to the

right, and he was breathing with the support of oxygen. His eyes were struggling to open, and in this battle for sight, he noticed him.

"Lord, have mercy!" he mumbled.

His heart beat rapidly, and his eyes uncontrollably welled up, thinking he angrily sent two men on their way, and this was the end. A man seated on the side of the bed stood. He was tall, about six feet and two inches, athletic, in his early fifties, quite refined, and clean-shaven with a light scent of expensive cologne. An oversized coat was laid neatly folded, with the lining exposed, across the chair with a hat and a pair of gloves perfectly atop. In low voices, the last two crucial people of Dan's vanishing life shook hands.

"Good evening. Pastor Haugen?"

"Yes."

"I am Nathan Horowitz. Nice to meet you and thank you for coming. I am Mr. Piattoni's attorney."

"Not a problem. Nice meeting you. This was not the way Dan had planned it. Mr. Peters died on impact, and Dan doesn't have long."

"Mr. Horowitz."

"Please, you can call me Nate."

"Nate, it was my understanding he is an atheist. Has he changed his mind and is confessing to God?"

"Oh! I don't believe so, Pastor Haugen."

"What a pity."

"What little I gathered from him, he met you yesterday?"

"Yes, this is true. When my family and I arrived at our home, their vehicle was stalled in front of our home. I offered them to come out of the cold and wait inside until the roadside service arrived. The weather worsened. It was getting late, and their service was delayed for hours, so quite naturally, we offered them a place for the night. Nothing more. We had the room—no inconvenience at all. This is awful, especially after I loaned them our truck that was involved in this terrible accident."

"No one ever predicts these things," Nate added.

Dan took a deep shallow breath and, in a hoarse tone, said, "Hello, Pastor!" He opened his right hand, gesturing him to come closer to his bedside.

"Does he know about Cane?" Pastor Haugen whispered.

"Yes! I told him."

He took a seat, and his eyes once again imploded in tears.

"Dan, I am genuinely sorry about all of this. Please forgive me for not being a better person, a better Christian."

Dan smiled and responded in a meek and trembling voice, "No, no, Pastor, none of this is your doing. I probably would have done the same if I were in your shoes. But you must know that Cane deliberately drove the truck off the road. He did this. He wanted us both dead."

"What? Cane? What are you saying?"

"Yes…yes he did."

"Oh my Lord, is there anything I can do for you? I know you were once a Christian. Please repent, confess, and say you believe in our Lord and Savior, Jesus. Dan, I will pray for you."

"No, and no need to apologize. Thank you for being so kind and inviting us to spend time with your beautiful family. Please forgive me for not being a better guest, and I'm sorry for causing so much trouble in your home. Tell Helen and the kids I said thank you."

Dan paused and breathed with extreme difficulty.

"Dan, it's all right."

Dan nodded and smiled.

"Give me your hands. Both of them, please."

He took both of his hands and placed them in Dan's hand.

"Dan, I want to pray for you now. Please. We must."

Nate walked over to the foot of the bed, and Dan slightly motioned his head in a downward nod at him. Nate reciprocated.

"Pastor, Paul had zeal, and God used him. You will do the right thing, and God will see to it."

"What? Do what, Dan? You do believe in God. Just say it. Repent, man. It's salvation. Say it, please."

With all of Dan's remaining strength, he squeezed Pastor Haugen's hands and, as he released them, along with his last breath. The heart-monitoring equipment flatlined, and the dreaded tone swelled through the room. Nate stood over Dan, kissed his forehead, and began to weep aloud.

"God, please have mercy on his soul," Pastor Haugen said as he gently placed Dan's hand across his stomach and continued to pray over him quietly.

"Good-bye, my dear friend. Good-bye. Everything is going to be okay now, I promise. Love you, Dan."

A nurse entered the room, and Dan's friends from the hallway anxiously followed. The nurse turned off the monitor, checked his pulse, and looked at the clock.

"I am sorry for your loss."

She turned off the IV, removed the patient chart, and, practically without notice, left the room. Pastor Haugen stepped back, allowing room for Dan's grief-stricken friends.

The female stood over the bed and flipped open her purse, nonchalantly retrieving a gold and black gaudy flask. She mused and removed the cap.

"Dan, here's to 'Evening Prayer.'"

She delicately kissed Dan on his lips and sipped another drink.

"I would offer you a drink. However, the bar is closed now. Yes, closed."

"Oh, Ingrid!" said Thomas, the older gentleman, scornfully.

Ingrid sat at the end of the bed and wept uncontrollably.

"Not like this! He did not plan it like this! Where are the best made plans now?" Thomas added.

"Oh, Dan. You wanted so badly to get to the healing home. He was trying to make it to the healing home. He would have been just fine had he made it. I know he would have. Our healing home!" Ingrid cried.

As his grieving friends moved toward Dan, Pastor Haugen discreetly stepped out and walked down the hall.

"Pastor Haugen!"

He turned, and it was Nate. "Hello, Nate. Surely you can understand me leaving. Too much has happened, and I can't seem to wrap my mind around it all. My heart grieves with you and the others right now. And Cane! What pushed him over the edge like this? A murder-suicide. This is unfathomable. You should be with the others."

"Pastor Haugen, a couple of times I've asked myself, is this a bad dream? And it's not. I understand your frustration and apprehension. I loved him, and we couldn't have been any closer if we were blood brothers. I'm heartbroken someone like Dan, who was so compassionate and peaceful, died by the hands of someone so heinous. This is the same person he bent over backward for as though he was his younger brother. Look how he repaid him," he said, pausing in-between weeping.

Pastor Haugen patted him on the back.

"I can't get over this. A murder-suicide, and for what?"

"No, it wasn't a murder-suicide."

"What did you say?"

"I've made promises to Dan I plan on keeping."

"Promises? You heard Dan—no, we heard Dan tell us with his own mouth that Cane did this."

"Pastor Haugen, I promised Dan on his deathbed I would never repeat this truth. As far as I'm concerned, what difference would it make? And I intend to honor one of his last requests. They're both gone, and that will not change. Keep it simple—a bad accident turned tragic."

"Man, you've got to be kidding me. As an attorney, what about withholding evidence? Aren't you obstructing justice?"

"I'm trying with everything in me not to say I could not care less what happened to Cane, but I will not. I'm mad as hell. Pardon! For whatever reason, Dan decided to change the ending to this story, so be it. I don't recall any murder-suicide conversation. In grief, it's common to speak out of terms."

"Dear God, man! You don't know what you're saying. You are speaking from a grieving heart."

"Pastor Haugen, there's so much more. It's rather complicated, and I will not take up much of your time. I'd like to talk to you about a very serious matter. Do you have time for a cup of coffee?"

"I think I need to leave here and get to my family, and you need to get back to the others. I told the police department I would stop by on my way home. They're expecting details as to how those two ended up with my truck. Listen to me. We're all a little shaken up here and in shock."

"You are correct. Yes, I understand fully. I'm only asking for a few more minutes."

"Very well."

Pastor Haugen hesitantly agreed, and the two took the elevator and headed down to the cafeteria. Nate bought coffee, and they located a vacant table.

"It's probably none of my business, but what happened last night? Why were you both so apologetic toward each other? Dan said something to me about the Rover breaking down."

"Yesterday, when my family and I arrived at our vacation home here, Dan's Range Rover had stalled just yards from our drive. I immediately noticed a small emergency orange cone behind the car, and Cane was standing near the front hood. Quite naturally, I stopped. Both of my sons, Andrew and Peter, we wanted to see if we could assist them in any way. As we walked toward the car, Dan got out and greeted us. Cane said he drove over some deep pothole a ways back. It started riding funny, a loud noise came from under the hood, and it stopped. They had been waiting for roadside assistance for forty-five minutes or so. Dan told us he owned a cabin about fifteen miles farther up the road. I was happy to meet someone else with property in the area. It was freezing outside, and I offered our place to stay until the tow arrived. They gladly accepted."

"That was a kind gesture, especially not knowing them."

"I introduced myself as Pastor Haugen, and Cane shook my hands with eagerness. The first thing he said was, 'I'm a Christian too!' I looked at Dan, and he shook his head, indicating no. I also noticed Cane was wearing a cross, and in my mind, this was a fellow saint we were helping. Helen, my wife, insisted they stay for dinner because the tow service called Dan and said they were short-handed and were experiencing a higher-than-normal amount of service calls. The snow started to really come down, and I suggested they stay with us until morning when things had cleared up. We had plenty of room, and after spending a little time with them, I didn't sense any type of danger to us. Everything was fine until Dan shared with us, including my kids, that he and Cane were gay. Not partners, but only friends. After that, it went south."

"Okaaay."

"I don't believe in homosexuality and will not bite my tongue on this. It's against God's written Word, and there was no way I was going to have two gay men sharing the same room in my home. A few heated conversations ensued, and it created an unpleasant situation. I dared not send them out in the middle of the night with blizzard conditions. I waited until morning and loaned them my truck. They left before my family got up."

"And what time was this?"

"Not quite six o'clock."

"So the accident occurred shortly afterward."

"I suppose so."

"Sorry to hear it ended on a bad note. I do appreciate you coming here, and not a moment too soon, may I add. Dan and I have been good friends for many years. There will never be another Dan, not in my lifetime. He is—was—the most generous, compassion-ate, and humbled person I've ever known."

"Okay, Nate, you now have my attention."

"It is imperative I shed some light as to who Dan truly was. At birth, he was adopted by a wealthy couple, Antonio and Luccia Piattoni, in their forties who loved and adored him. They were devout Catholics, and Dan was raised a Catholic. The Piattonis traveled extensively abroad and lived a privileged life. He had a nanny and attended the best schools. Well, his second year at Stanford University, Dan came home for spring break, and dur-ing dinner with his parents and aunt, he dropped the bomb—that is, he's gay. What a firestorm! His father was devastated and ada-mantly believed it was a phase orchestrated by a mental deficiency. He proposed an extensive psychiatric treatment at a facility in Switzerland, but Dan refused. This refusal outraged his father, who gave him an ultimatum of disinheritance. He stood his ground and lost his financial support. Not immediately, but later in that year, he dropped out of Stanford with nowhere to go.

"God bless his mother. She secretly supported him, and he believed his father had knowledge of this. She continued to love and care for him despite her disagreeing with his choice to become gay. The alienation and her secrecy proved too much for her. She told his father she would never forgive him and grieved herself into illness—literally to death. His father declined to allow Dan to attend her funeral. Based on what Dan shared with me, he never was able to heal emotionally from not seeing his mother toward the end of her life. Never! Yes, they met secretly, but she became bedridden prior to her death. It was a dark, dark time in his life, and he admitted to behaving irresponsibly and recklessly with some of his personal choices."

Nate paused, took a handkerchief from his pocket, wiped his tears, and continued.

"Dan's mother had no siblings, and his father had one younger sister, Sovenia. She married at a very young age, and her husband was killed in the Second World War. Dan could not recall if he overheard a conversation between his parents when he was younger, or if he always believed in the back of his mind that his Aunt Sovenia was his biological mother and that he looked just like her. She had a couple of mental breakdowns, but all in all she was endearing and always instructing him about life. As a matter of fact, she was a concert pianist."

"Wow! Dan had an interesting yet seriously privileged life."

"Yes, he did, and, trust me, it gets better."

"Out of curiosity, how did Dan's father obtain his wealth?"

"Early on, he invested in real estate all over the place. Here and in Europe. Obviously, Mr. Piattoni was a sharp business tycoon. Dan said his father proudly spoke frequently about looking forward to passing on the legacy of wealth to his grandchildren. Sadly, Dan's father suffered a debilitating massive stroke and passed away almost one year to the day of his wife's death anniversary. I mean, almost to the day. Dan attended the funeral with his Aunt Sovenia. Remember, it gets better."

"Really?"

"His father did remove him from the will as he stated, but left practically everything to his unpredictable sister, Sovenia. In retrospect, there was more to that decision, but such as it is, we'll never know. Prior to her total mental demise, she requested Dan to meet her with the attorneys at a well-known law firm in San Francisco. At the meeting, she legally reinstated his wealth, and he became the sole beneficiary of the Piattoni fortune. The day he became a millionaire, he lost his Aunt Sovenia, who could have very well been his mother, She hung herself. Distraught and truthfully all alone, he decided to honor a family secret about his identity. He traveled to his family home in Nice and resided there for four and a half years before settling back in San Francisco. Somewhere between losing his mother and returning to the States, he abandoned his faith and became an atheist.

I first met Dan when I was working pro bono at the law firm. He arrived early for the meeting with his Aunt Sovenia. While he was waiting, I graciously offered him a cup of coffee and a small talk. I had heard a few stories about his parents, the situation, and felt sorry for the guy. He asked how old I was, and we joked about being the same age. When he returned to San Francisco, he requested I assist him, and the rest is history. He remembered our conversation, and to think a cup of coffee separated me from the others."

"Please forgive me if I offend you, but are you gay?"

"No! No! I'm happily married to my wife, Deidre, and we have twin girls, Natasha and Nadia. Dan attended our wedding, and he was there to support me during their birth. He was their godfather, and they called him Uncle Dan. An awful case of the flu is the only reason Deidre is not here. You may or may not understand, but I was truly traditional in his life, a good ole American traditional family."

"Hmmm. I am married with three teenagers—two boys and one girl. My wife's name is Helen. I have to tell you, the kids really were drawn to Cane, almost like a big brother. They were planning to go skiing and hunt for rabbit."

"I'm being very serious here. Was Dan a true die-hard atheist?"

"Are you kidding me? Very much so! There is no easy explanation. Believe me, Dan and I went around in circles on this one."

Pastor Haugen shook his head.

"Just curious, when both of his parents and his aunt passed away, did he pursue trying to find out who his biological parents were? He certainly had the means."

"I distinctly remember suggesting to him to put some things to rest, especially when his Aunt Sovenia passed away. Do you know what his response was? 'The truth will not change the direction of the wind.' Dan was accustomed to secrets his entire life, and at the end of it, he continued. Pastor Haugen, Dan asking me to let Cane's ultimate criminal act rest wasn't unusual for him. It's one more thing that speaks to who he was. He said Cane's parents deserved a more respectable ending to their only son's life. I kid you not. In his own way, he had forgiven him."

"I'm taken aback by all of this."

"Pastor Haugen, with Dan's multiple sclerosis and AIDS attacking his failing health, he only had a few months, if not weeks, to live."

"What? Is that why the older gentleman upstairs said he didn't plan the end like this? I thought to myself no one plans their death."

"You do if you realize you're dying."

"True."

"He planned to go to his family's Tahoe vacation home for a last retreat to sort some business out undisturbed and return home for the remaining time of his life. I urged Dan to hire a nurse, but he insisted on his new charity case, Cane Peters."

"New charity case?"

"Their acquaintance was relatively new. I met the train wreck, and my gut instinct was right. I just couldn't put my finger on it. Several months ago, Dan was out having dinner alone in one of his favorite spots in Sausalito. The entire restaurant, I suppose, overheard Cane and a friend, roommate or something, engage in a nasty fight. He was being kicked out on his butt, clothes on the curb and all, and Cane was yelling about being broke and having no place to go. Of course, no place to go resonated with Dan. He handed the waiter a note to hand to Cane. After reading the note, he was belligerent and walked over to the table and accused Dan of thinking he was a prostitute. He tried to explain to him how he wanted to genuinely help him, that he understood firsthand what it's like to have no place to go to. Cane pretended he was too outraged to listen and left."

"Pretended?"

"Yes, pretended! As Dan was approaching his car, he showed up out of nowhere and scared him to death. The young fool."

"You didn't care for the young man at all, did you?"

"Not at all. Dan omitted no details telling me how they met. Anyway, Cane asked Dan if the offer was still open. Now that took some serious nerve. But Dan, being the person he was, said yes and took him in the following day.

His illnesses were quite taxing on him, and he was gradually breaking down. It was so bad that he began a cannabis treatment, which he swore worked."

"Cannabis treatment? Marijuana?"

"Yes, and please don't judge him."

Pastor Haugen put both hands up to gesture in agreement.

"His days were indeed numbered. Believe me when I say he had friends who would have assisted him around the clock, but, for the life of me, I don't understand why or what he saw in Cane. Oh, Dan was no one's fool. Early the next morning, he e-mailed me the information Cane provided him about himself. Born in Kentucky, being in San Francisco for less than a year, etcetera."

"What did you find out about him?"

"Plenty to know he had some serious issues. Cane told Dan part of the truth, and I gathered the entire truth after my investigation."

"Was he some sort of criminal?"

"No way. As a matter of fact, his name was Jeffrey Cane Peters. In his hometown, they called him Jeff. When he moved out here, he went by the name of Cane. Our investigator discovered a little scandal involving him. Again, my friend Dan was being drawn in quickly by this young man, and I expeditiously needed solid information."

"Nate, I didn't sense any problem with either one of them. We enjoyed their company so much that we invited them to stay for dinner. It only digressed when Dan told us they were gay but not partners, only friends. It was then that Cane seemed agitated with Dan when he told us. No, I am certain he was agitated."

"Let me explain something, Pastor Haugen. You see, Dan proudly came out, and Cane was horribly found out. Huge difference here. Huge. Even in this culture of acceptance, it still requires strength to come out as a gay person. Freedom to be recognized and respected for who you are is essential to surviving."

"Nate, you have my heartfelt sympathy for your loss. I know the man lying upstairs was a dear friend and impacted your life considerably. However, I remain steadfast that homosexuality is a sin against God's law. And, frankly, I'm not interested in homosexuality's unwritten rules and regulations of acceptance. Not at all! Not to be rude or mean-spirited, but merely stating a fact."

"Pastor Haugen, I did not ask you for coffee to argue your point."

"So what's the urgency?"

"I needed to share this crucial information with you. Paint a picture. It is crucial to know a little history about them. Please trust me on this!"

"If you say so, you have my undivided attention."

"My personal opinion is I don't believe Cane was altogether gay, if that makes sense."

"Not really. That's like saying a woman can't be a little pregnant. Either she is or she isn't. Don't you agree?"

"I wish it were just that simple. I believe in his drunken stupor, he somehow became entangled in a weird situation. He was born and raised in a well-respected Southern Baptist family from Kentucky. Both his parents are still living there, and he has a twin sister, Jennifer. Oh, this gets really interesting. He was getting married to a lovely young woman from another respectable family. Yes, a woman! Her name was Emma Tollison. They dated close to two years prior to becoming engaged. Both of their families were ecstatic and supportive of the young couple. The night before his wedding during his bachelor party at a hotel in Oldham County,

Kentucky, he was caught in an intimate posture in the restroom with another man—a popular gay guy."

"A popular who?"

"A very well-known gay guy. No one knows how the two met or why this man was at the hotel. There are rumors this guy was on the prowl and was a gold digger seeking to hit the lottery at this bachelor party."

"What? At a Christian bachelor party? Am I disconnected with this culture or what?"

"The world is full of people desperate to push their agenda, and he had one. Please hear the rest. Cane swore his innocence and claimed intoxication, someone putting something in his drink, and adamantly denied ever being involved in anything like that, but the bull was already out the gate. Photos popped up on social media, and the rest is history. He irrefutably lost his reputation, fiancée, and both families were distraught. His would be father-in-law had already invested ninety-five thousand dollars in the wedding, and both families put together a sizeable down payment for their first home as a special wedding gift. The couple was going to have an excellent jump start. That was an indication how much everyone was looking forward to this union.

Cane relocated to the San Francisco, where no one knew him, area to escape his tragedy. He fell completely off the radar. It wasn't long before he had a reputation of being moody, quick-tempered, definitely no drugs but drinks a lot, and acts like an absolute imbecile. Back in Kentucky, it's like we're not talking about the same guy. The investigation concluded he was a model straight citizen, straight to the core. He was hardworking and dedicated to their church youth ministries his entire life, and there was absolutely nothing to indicate misconduct and, here's the bombshell, nothing to indicate he was a homosexual. I believe the choice he made drinking heavily that night was an automatic deal breaker and cost him dearly. Poor guy's life went completely downhill. No surprise to me he had so many issues."

"Wow! Why didn't Cane get involved with a church in the city? The pieces are starting to come together. Cane was humiliated and hurt. This caused him to be so angry and volatile. Initially, when we met Cane, he was sincere, polite, and super easy to talk to, but when Dan exposed the fact that they were gay, he shut down and gradually turned into someone else different. Oh, yes, I experienced his anger. I remember saying to myself, how could he be this seemingly nice young man and then the next minute turn into a person that loathes me? I will not disagree with you. Maybe he had a personality disorder, but, perhaps, misdirected and unresolved personal issues were at the root of all his problems. He lost the woman he loved and was most likely accused of living a double life."

"Dan confided in me that he made several attempts to discuss his past, but he always became angry and refused to talk about it. Cane reminded Dan on a couple of occasions to remember he was hired to assist him, and prying into his personal life was not part of the deal. Get this—Dan went as far as to share with him the time in his life when he came out and was disinherited and isolated afterward. He was hoping to foster an environment of trust so Cane would open up and begin the healing process. The real sadness in all of this is that the young man had no idea my dear, dear friend lying dead upstairs knew everything. I mean everything! And he never uttered a word because he wanted to spare him some sense of dignity. Those were his exact words, and again this speaks to who he was—a compassionate, sensitive, and respectful person to everyone.

The only time Dan noticed a sparkle of hope was when Cane went with him to see the families in the shelters. He said Cane was a natural, and everyone, especially the youth, warmed up to him. He was in his element helping and encouraging them."

"I don't understand why he didn't seek refuge or help from one of the local congregations. Maybe he thought his past would be exposed. Cane lost the battle with his personal demons. The last words the young man uttered before leaving our home troubled me. He said, 'Before a person can make an exodus, he must first have entered.' He said it twice."

"What do you think he meant by that?"

Standing with arms folded, he replied, "The jury is still out on this one, but I believe I know what he meant."

"I'd like to know."

"Based on what you've told me, Cane wasn't totally gay. Yes, he engaged in a despicable sexual act and was branded. He may have been set up, for all we know. He couldn't exodus because he had never entered. Get it? He never entered homosexuality, so there was no need to exit."

"That's a stretch. Why did he allow Dan to identify him as gay?"

"What makes people do strange things? Cane desperately needed a Christian confidante, not a wealthy atheist. He was drawn into your friend's world out of convenience, and again that cost him. Making one poor decision after another seldom, if ever, ends well."

"As I said, Dan tried to be that confidante. Had he opened up to him, he would have found a compassionate person willing to listen and offer solid advice. Knowing Dan, he probably would have suggested Cane return home to his family and face his fears."

"Hmmm."

"Pastor Haugen, I left my phone upstairs, and I need to check on everyone and call Deidre. Would you please wait here for just a little bit long? I promise to wrap this up."

"I need to check on Helen and the kids myself. I'll be here."

Nate partially smiled and left.

Pastor Haugen realized he had, on so many levels, failed Cane, and his contempt toward homosexuality blindsided his ability to minister to a hurting young Christian. If he wasn't gay, why didn't he just come out and say he wasn't? This outcome could have been different. The bickering at the house, the accident, and now hearing about their personal lives were a "road to Damascus" experience. The Rover breaking down in front of their home out of all the places in Tahoe was no small accident.

In his penitent state, he asked God to forgive him once more for being so angry and not recognizing a deeply disturbed soul. He remembered thinking to himself as they unloaded the bags how this handsome young man was so polite and jovial. It now all had come together and made perfect sense.

He recalled noticing a subtle shock from Cane when Dan stated they were gay, apparently hitting him from the blind side. Taking matters from bad to worse, their expressions of disappointment took him right back to Kentucky, and his subdued paralyzing emotions surfaced into a layered miasma of untreated pain. Too long he was strangled by fear, which caused him to shrivel into a heartbreaking defeat.

Dan, you foolish, foolish man. What on earth was going through your mind? he thought. What did he want to accomplish? Was it an impulsive act to test Cane's manhood to see firsthand if he would step up to the plate or step out? Cane was too vulnerable.

Returning to the present, Pastor Haugen thought of how pointless it was to continually overanalyze the complexities of this situation as he surrendered to the truth of never knowing.

THE ULTIMATE APPEAL

As Nate entered Dan's room, the whispers ceased, and all eyes shadowed him—Ingrid's, Thomas's, and Jonathan's. Shrugging his shoulders, he took a seat in the chair and supported his head with both hands. For a brief moment, he was tempted to share the dark secret of how Dan and Cane died, but he realized it was one of Dan's last wishes, and there could be endless repercussions. Not to mention a potential scandal would brew and wreak havoc. He was hoping Pastor Haugen would honor Dan's request and allow Cane's parents to bury their son in peace.

Thomas Lee Seymore, the older gentleman comforting Ingrid earlier, was a retired music schoolteacher. He volunteered at music departments and organizations with inspiring students. Many kids in the area benefited from their combined efforts in obtaining quality instruments.

Ingrid Livingston was, perhaps, other than Nate, one of Dan's beloved friends who owned a small boutique in Sausalito and met him during one of his many fundraisers. She offered to take a leave and care for him, and as expected he emphatically refused. She, on the other hand, assuredly believed in God, but not institutionalized religion, which provided her a reason not to attend worship; she didn't trust people. This introverted behavior gave way to absolute control of her interaction with people.

Jonathan Murphy had been Dan's neighbor since he moved into the neighborhood. He was outgoing and lacked any trace of shyness. The commonality here was classical music. Jonathan considered himself an authority on famous past and current harpist. Dan recruited Jonathan to provide the music for most of his fundraisers.

"Where have you been?" asked Thomas.

"I was with Pastor Haugen."

"Please, for goodness' sake, no one get offended here, but did Dan request a pastor on his deathbed?"

"No. I mean, yes. Well, yes and no."

"Make up your mind, Nate. Which is it?" asked Ingrid.

"Let me explain. Dan's Range Rover broke down yesterday in front of Pastor Haugen's home. They had been sitting there for about forty-five minutes or so when he and his family arrived for their vacation. They offered their home to Dan and Cane while they waited for roadside assistance. It started getting late, so they stayed for dinner. The weather changed for the worst, and so the pastor suggested they spend the night. Around six, they borrowed his pickup truck to head out to Dan's place, and somewhere between there, the accident occurred."

"Strange set of events here. He is going to be sorely missed. Look how he touched all of our lives," said Jonathan.

"Nate, you are fortunate Dan lived long enough to speak to you and the pastor. Poor Cane died at the scene. Oh my God! What about his family? Did he have any family?" added Ingrid.

"Yes. I notified his parents this afternoon. They are beyond devastated. Cane has a twin sister, Jennifer, and we spoke. I put her in touch with my office so we can get them out here as soon as possible and then charter a plane to Tahoe."

"You know, that sounds like something Dan would have done. He believed in Cane despite his funky attitude at times. I remember when I first met Cane and how unnecessarily rude he was to me. Dan always said without fail to give him time. Right! I am still convinced that young man had secrets. We'll never know now," said Thomas.

"Dan and I knew about Cane's family from day one. We never let on, and that's the way Dan wanted it."

"This is like a terrible dream! I just know if he had made it to the healing home, it would have been okay. Oh, God, he was trying to make it to the healing home." Ingrid lamented.

"I left Pastor Haugen downstairs, and I need to call Deidre. I'll be back shortly."

Nate went down the hall and located a quiet corner where he called Deidre with the news of Dan and Cane and then informed her of his decision to remain in Tahoe until tomorrow.

Upon returning to the cafeteria, he noticed Pastor Haugen on the phone, and he gestured him to come over.

"Helen, Nate is here. I'll call when I'm on my way. Don't worry, I will. Love you too. How's it going upstairs?"

"Everyone is in disbelief, and poor Ingrid, she's lost her best friend. And they were shocked to learn Cane had family. Of course, I've known all the while, but still, his being introverted is baffling to all."

"Nate, I've had some time to think about this entire situation, and I have my own theory. Number one, Cane was, without doubt, a Christian. We unconditionally received him, and he related to us because we reminded him of his own family. Number two, this raised major issues with your friend because he, on the other hand, was an outsider, and Cane was totally the opposite around Dan's camp. Number three, Dan called this vulnerable young man out on the carpet about his homosexuality. And lastly, there was a heated argument when they left our home, and only God knows what was said between those two. I'm convinced Dan hit a nerve, and it caused Cane to snap. Helen was awakened by their arguing when they left. I drowned out whatever was going on."

"When I spoke to Dan alone, I asked him what happened. He admitted he pushed Cane too hard and hinted he knew about his scandal in Kentucky."

"Oh, no. No!"

"Dan admitted to me that he asked Cane if he hated him or hated the fact he was gay. Cane did not answer, but instead he drove the car off the ravine."

"Dear God. What a horrible, horrible experience. God knows I'm not off the hook. I have to live with the fact that I turned my back on him and said some pretty severe things, which his own father, being a pastor, I'm sure told him."

"If you had to do it all over again. Would you say and do the same?"

"Definitely."

"Then there you have it. You made a decision based on the information or circumstances that were before you."

"Spoken like a true attorney."

"No. Those are the facts. You and your family made an indelible impression on Dan, especially when you hear what I have to tell you."

"Man, this day keeps getting interesting! Dan and Cane were both good people who, for all intents and purposes, should have never agreed to work together. I believe Cane would have found himself again. San Francisco was, perhaps, not the best place to redeem himself. I'm speaking in terms of how he was raised and what he was accustomed to spiritually. That young man desperately needed his family."

"Dan knew the last days of his life would be spent in bed. The only thing he got wrong on this one, it was in a hospital and not at home."

"Poor guy."

"He was finalizing the Luccia House—respectfully named after his beloved mother."

"The Luccia House?"

"The majority of gays don't have children and, in a lot of cases, no one to care for them in their aging years. There are years, if not decades, people spend isolated from their original family and friends. The Luccia House is a place where those who are terminally ill or alone can live in a comfortable, safe, and in a like-minded environment. This is a multimillion-dollar project slated to begin sometime this year."

"Wow! In San Francisco?"

"No. The purchased property is right outside of San Francisco in Tiburon. Dan sold most of his real estate holding to raise funds for this project."

"With his passing, are you now going to see this through?"

"Funny you should ask. My part is to distribute the funds as the overseeing attorney, but someone else will totally be in charge of the final design, establishing a board, hiring of staff, crew, etcetera. It will be an enormous undertaking. We're talking about a forty-four-million-dollar project."

"Forty-four million dollars!"

"Correct."

"That's a substantial amount of money."

"You see, when word got out about the Luccia House, you can well imagine people from everywhere wanted to be a part of this meaningful project. Keep in mind, only his friends in his inner circle knew he had a short time to live, with the exception of Cane. As I mentioned, Dan began the aggressive cannabis treatment when he was diagnosed with MS, which came on later. Cane assumed it was the MS, not AIDS. He was growing weaker, and it became increasingly difficult for him to determine who would be worthy of fulfilling his dream his way. Make no mistake, he loved all his dear friends, but he was struggling with this decision. He knew them too well, not in any bad sense, but he wanted exact influences.

"I made a solemn promise to Dan I intend to keep. His wish was to die at home peacefully. However, he obstinately as well as legally instructed me that in the event his business was not totally in order on his deathbed, whoever's hands he held with both of his hands, he would nod, and I would reciprocate with a nod, and this was the appointed person of the Luccia House. It doesn't get any simpler than that, and this is specified in his will. Before you showed up, I was almost convinced he would pass on before assigning this brilliant dream to anyone."

Pastor Hague looked perplexed, and he began to appear stunned.

"Yes, you are the one Dan appointed to take over the Luccia House. Congratulations."

"Oh, no, no, no. Stop yourself. I'm not the person, and thank you, but no thank you. I remember him nodding at you, and that's between you and him."

"You're kidding, right? Did you hear me? You are the one to manage this multimillion-dollar project. This is huge! Do you know the people who would give anything to be in your shoes? I told you I am the overseeing attorney, and I will be there to assist you through this entire process and upon completion."

"Honestly, I'm sad to say, but you've just wasted both of our valuable time if this is what you've held me up for. Your close friend just passed away, and his grieving close friends are upstairs. You should be having this conversation with one or all of them, not me! I'm a pastor, and must I say this again, I don't believe in homosexuality at all. I don't plan to waver from this position. Not at all."

"This doesn't have anything to do with homosexuality in its entirety. It's about helping people in need who are alone and can live their lives out in a comfortable and loving place."

"Listen to yourself. Nothing to do with homosexuality. No, nothing is further from the truth. Are you kidding me? Nate, come on! Who are we kidding here? It has everything to do with homosexuality. Wow! Last I checked, homosexuality includes gays, lesbians, transgenders, and confused men with mustaches and beards wearing lipstick and high heels. Man, I can't believe you. You'd say anything to push your agenda. It was a pleasure meeting you, but my work here is done. Why are you so adamant about telling me all of this, especially now?"

"Please! Please, Pastor Hague. I employ you to hear me out. Just hear me out! He only knew you for a short period of time, but my God, man, something compelled him to believe in you. He believed in you! To me, I see it as a miracle. Something awesome. He was an atheist, but he left this to you—a pastor, a God-fearing, believing Christian. Dan knew you were on your way, and I know with every fiber in me that he held on until you arrived by his side. He held on for you! I'm speaking the truth. Not his three dear friends upstairs. You! I'm not lying or twisting his words. He took both of your hands—none of his waiting friends. It was you."

Pastor Hague took a deep breath, released a calm sigh, and sat down.

"My heart goes out to anyone who has to die alone and in pain. I honestly can't envision such an ordeal. I'm humbled and honored that Dan would consider me, but I must obstinately decline. I can't. I'm absolutely overwhelmed with everything. Can't you see this is too much right now? One minute I'm entertaining two guests in my home, it turned into a hostile situation, I loaned them my truck because I literally wanted them gone, and they both died in a murder-suicide in the truck. Dear God! Yes, a murder-suicide. I need to get back to my wife and kids."

"Pastor Hague, this has been an exasperating last twenty-four hours. I've lost one of my dearest friends and my daughter's godfather. This is a tough place to be in for all of us. I chose to tell now while it was fresh on your mind. Who's to say if we had this same conversation in a few weeks that you'd remember anything? We are all in utter shock! It has been my experience that shock does strange things to the mind. Being forgetful or spacing out is way at the top of the list. Hear me out before you say definitively no. Take as long as you need and discuss it with your wife and kids. Later on after you've had an opportunity to recover a bit from this, you may feel quite differently. Don't forget, I'm a Christian too.

"I didn't have any gay friends until I met Dan. Let's face it. My mindset was like most people—a bit homophobic. Our relationship grew from a business to a respectful friendship. Never once did he disrespect my boundaries, my family, or ever attempt to force his way of thinking on us. My ten-year-old girls don't know their godfather was gay."

"Now I must draw a line in the sand. Guess what, Nate? I'm not a homophobic. I am a hellphobic. Hellphobic! I have a deep fear and contempt for hell, so being a hellphobic is at the top of my list, and from one Christian to another, it should be at the top of yours. No compromising on this one."

"Pastor Haugen, I see I have offended you, and I apologize, but it is what it is here."

"Nate, hell is what it is, and it will outlive homosexuality by eternity."

"Again, my intent is not to offend."

"We've spent all this time discussing Dan. What about Cane and his family? We can't dismiss him, regardless of his insidious actions. I have sons, and Cane weighs heavily on my heart. He was so young. His parents must be devastated, and his father is a pastor too! My God."

"His parents and twin sister are taking a red-eye tonight and then flying here shortly afterward. My office is making all the arrangements, and they will be staying at one of the hotels nearby. If losing their son isn't enough, I found out there was no communication whatsoever from Cane since he left almost a year ago. This epitomizes unfinished business."

"None?"

Nate nodded.

"I can't speak for you, but this is a wake-up call for me as a parent. I pray to God that none of my kids will ever do anything to cause such a family riff and shut down communication like that. Satan is always the author of confusion and destruction. Look what his handiwork accomplished."

"Is it Satan, or human stubbornness?"

"You know the answer to this one—pride of life! It's Satan."

"Pastor Haugen, I'm hopeful after a few hours of rest you'll seriously reconsider the Luccia House. I'm too exhausted to push this issue with you. Thank you again for your time and being so kind to Dan, and, yes, Cane. I need to get back to Dan so we can make arrangements to get him home now."

"Nate, would you please have the Peters get in touch with me when they arrive?"

"Sure thing. As I alluded, a tragic accident."

"I believe the Peters would enjoy dinner with us, and the kids especially can share with them the last few hours of Cane's life prior to everything going awry. It is the least I can do. He was a good young man, and it's none of my business how, who, and what went wrong. I will make certain they know how he spoke with pride about his family, church, and community. Nothing more! 'Light in a messenger's eyes brings light to the heart, and good news gives health to the bones.' Proverbs chapter fifteen, verse thirty. Mr. Horowitz, Lord willing, I will be talking to you soon."

"Please."

Pastor Haugen left the building after the two embraced. Nate sat at the table and was utterly consumed with anguish as he laid his head on his folded arms and wept aloud.

NIGHTMARE'S OVERTURE

Pastor Haugen stopped by the South Lake Tahoe Police Department to offer a statement. He told the police detective that Dan's Range Rover had some problems and stopped in front of their vacation home. What followed was inviting the two inside, they stayed for dinner, the weather taking a turn for the worst, they spent the night and left early the next morning in his pickup truck. The detective asked if there were possibly any mechanical problems with the truck, and he responded that, to his knowledge, there weren't any issues.

How can I leave this place and not mention what Dan told us on his deathbed? Am I now guilty of withholding crucial evidence? God, should I turn around and say, "Oh, I forgot to tell you that Dan told his attorney and a pastor friend that Cane deliberately caused this tragedy." An attorney and a pastor, how can you go wrong there? God, please guide me into your truths. Tell me what to do. As he started the car to leave the police department, a verse echoed over his spirit—"All things are lawful, but not all things are not expedient...all things are lawful, but not all things are not expedient" (1 Cor. 10:23).

He smiled and said aloud, "Thank you, God, for always being right on time. Bless your holy name. For now, I'll be silent."

Pastor Haugen's prayer was answered in that moment. God did not desire for him to tarry needlessly. God will never tempt his people to do wrong, but will test them to do right. Satan, on the other hand, will tempt you always to do wrong and never do right. "When tempted, no one should say, 'God is tempting me.' For God cannot be tempted by evil, nor does he tempt anyone; but each person is tempted when they are dragged away by their own evil desire and enticed" (James 1:13–14). Regardless of our walk, whether three months or three decades, we will, without fail, continuously encounter circumstances that challenge who we are at our core spiritual being—result of a fallen world. The beauty of Pastor Haugen's dependent relationship with God was that he understood he is human, not above reproach or sin, and God's counsel alone for him was a way of life.

Driving toward their home, he decided to go farther up the road and visit the crash site first. It was less than fifteen miles up the road. As he approached the area, from a distance, the yellow caution tape bordered the embankment. Oversized tire tracks mixed with normal tread marks separated the snow from the road. As he parked and exited his vehicle, a calm eeriness permeated the air. He walked and peered cautiously over the edge to see a freshly damaged ponderosa pine tree, and his eyes welled up as he stood in silence. Thoughts spiraled in and out from words to moments, moments to words of the last sixteen hours.

"Cane and Dan, may God have mercy on your souls. Cane, so many of us failed you. All you needed to do was hang on a little while longer, and God would have shown you the way out of the darkness. I'm sure of it—he always does. Why couldn't you have just hung on? I'm so sorry. Dan, what did you say to Cane? Cane, was it so terrible that you couldn't walk away? Only God knows."

Pastor Haugen returned to his car and sat, staring aimlessly. Moments later, he nodded into sleep. The jerking of his head awakened him, and it was time for him to go to bed in the safety of his home and not become a fatality himself. Looking out of his left side mirror to make a U-turn, he instead drove up the road. Out of absolute curiosity, he was in search of Dan's home. When the kids were asking how to get there, he remembered Dan describing a hunter green and black mailbox on a four-foot black brick stand with a large iron green letter P on each side at the end of the drive. Minutes later, the large P was recognizable in the distance.

The cleared driveway, in all likelihood, was done by the maintenance person yesterday prior to their expected arrival. The home was nestled among ponderosa and fir pine trees. A large beautiful window showcased this home with rustic character, hand-peeled log accents, and a wraparound porch. Dan was modest in the description of size and quality of this trilevel home.

Walking up to the house, he saw that a focal point was the overhead wood etched sign, "Welcome to the Healing Home." Pastor Haugen began to laugh aloud.

"Dan, I guess we all had the same idea. Now I see why you laughed when you saw our 'Welcome to Blue Castle.' You laughed at mine, now I'm laughing at yours. Great minds do think alike. I'm sure your mother was responsible for this one, and Helen for ours. Daniel Piattoni, you had a good and interesting life, man. Cane would have gotten himself together here too had we—yes, I said we—given him half the chance. I feel it right here."

He took a tour of the grounds and noticed the boat ramp. During a conversation with Dan after dinner, he proudly described the 1946 Chris Classic boat that was in a nearby storage facility. He said it was one of his father's favorite toys. Pastor Haugen concluded this would be the only time he was able to spend here, so he sat on the front steps, contently smiling.

"Mrs. Piattoni, you left a legacy here, and your son has asked me to help carry it out. Yes, me, Pastor Anders Haugen. What are the odds? The Luccia House—your house. Why did Dan ask me? Though we do have a small roadblock—homosexuality. God in heaven knows I'm not going to waver not one blessed inch. So where does that leave your Luccia House for the ailing and aged gays?"

His phone rang, and it was Helen, worried about him.

"Hey, babe! Tired. Dog-tired. I'm not too far away, and I should be there in about fifteen minutes or so. Where are the kids? Great! Before I forget to tell you, Cane's parents and a twin sister will be here tomorrow some time. I think we should invite them over for dinner. I knew you'd agree. Yes, and there's more. You'll need to be sitting down. I'll fill you in later. No, no. Wait until I get back. See you soon. Love you too!"

In that moment, he decided not to share with Helen Cane's deliberate criminal act. Nate wasn't going to divulge this truth and most assuredly would take it to his grave. Yes, a tragic accident for now.

"God, give me strength to make it home safely. I can hardly see straight."

Dan stood and took one more look at the Healing Home and then headed down the road. In the distance, he saw Joe Martin with a tow bed parked in front of the Range Rover. Joe walked toward the drive to meet him.

"Evening Pastor Haugen."

"Hey, Joe. Good to see you. How's it going?"

"Just fine, sir."

"So you're here to tow the Range Rover?"

"Yes, sir. An attorney by the name of Nathaniel Horowitz contacted me and said the owner had passed away in that accident this morning, and he wanted me to get it off the road and to the yard. I heard the call over the radio, and when I got there, I recognized your pickup right away. My heart started beating something crazy 'cause I thought it was you and one of your sons. Sure glad it wasn't. Well, you know what I mean. I'm not glad it was them either. That didn't come out right."

"No need to explain, Joe. I understand exactly what you're saying."

"Good friends of yours?"

"I knew them."

"Pastor Haugen, maybe the young man was trying to avoid hitting a deer or something and lost control. That can happen. Terrible way to go, but in my line of business, you see it all."

"Oh, yes."

"Terrible this happened to your friends."

"I agree."

"Their vehicle broke down, and you loaned them yours?"

Pastor Haugen nodded.

"Anyone would have done the same. Well, when it's your time to go, it's just your time. Listen to me carrying on. Pastor Haugen, good seeing you, and please give my best to your lovely wife and family."

"Will do, and thanks, Joe."

"Thank you. I'm just doing what I enjoy. Do you know if they thoroughly checked under the hood when it stopped here?"

"I'm sure they did. Why?"

"I called that attorney before you drove up and told him there is absolutely nothing wrong with this here Range Rover."

"What? Nothing wrong. It stalled right here."

"I couldn't find anything wrong. It started right up, smooth as a top. No hesitation at all. Quite naturally, I checked under the hood and could not locate any problems there either. I'm going to take it back to the yard and wait until this attorney gives me instructions where he wants it delivered in San Francisco. Top-of-the-line Range Rover too."

"I'm sure."

"Take care."

"You too, Joe!"

Pastor Haugen was in disbelief hearing there was nothing wrong with the Rover. Nothing wrong whatsoever. He thought how circumstance after circumstance was becoming unbelievable by the minute. Cane said it wouldn't even turn over. The indicator lights were on, and he tried it again when they unloaded the truck with the boys. What was going on here?

Helen opened the door and stood waiting with TJ. "Hey, Anders. Is that Joe down there?"

"Oh, yes. What a day. I mean, what a day. Where do I begin?"

"That interesting?"

As he walked around the car, he said, "Get this! Joe said there is absolutely nothing wrong with that truck. Nada! Starts up smooth as a top! Unbelievable!"

"Maybe it was running hot or something?"

"Yeah, right. Dan and Cane told us the indicator lights were on, and it wouldn't make a sound."

"You're tired. Don't read too much into that. There could be a thousand and one reasons why it's working now."

"Helen!"

"Okay, Anders. Don't read too much into what is going on."

"Hey, TJ. Didn't mean to ignore you." He reached down and rubbed TJ's back.

"Honey, I need to get some rest. I can barely keep my eyes open. Where are the kids?"

"All inside waiting on you. Wait a minute, no hug or anything?"

"Sorry, I'm out of it!"

"Hey there, Haugenbunch!"

Sarah got up and hugged him. "Hey, Dad. How's it going?"

"Glad to be home. Everyone okay?"

"Sure," said Peter.

"I'm good," added Andrew.

"Okay, we'll talk later after I shower, eat a little something, and rest. Afterward, I'll fill everyone in with what's going on and what to expect over the next few days. Believe me when I say you'll get an earful."

Helen knew her husband was suffering from sheer fatigue, and a rested father was much more discerning in a discussion with three curious outspoken teenagers. He went into the bedroom and closed the door.

"Mom, what's really going on with Dad?"

"Andrew, two men died in the truck. He's been at the hospital meeting with Dan's attorney and friends. He had to give a statement at the police station, and it doesn't stop there. Cane's parents and his twin sister will be arriving tomorrow, and your dad plans to invite them over for dinner. If the day wasn't over, he ran into Joe Martin a few minutes ago, and he was told there is nothing wrong with Dan's truck and that it started right up."

"Ah, man, that's crazy."

"Your dad's tired, and his heart is heavy. He needs a few hours of undisturbed sleep, and then with a rested mind and body, he can sort this out with us. We'll eventually start our vacation, but we've got to work through these challenges. Cane's family will need our support, and Dan has no relatives, only close friends. We will be there for them as well! Remember, none of this caught God by surprise, only us. Try to keep the commotion at a minimum, please. Okay?"

"We've got this, Mom," Peter added.

"Good!"

"Why don't you all take TJ out for a bit? I'm sure he'd love it."

"Okay, Mom!" replied Andrew.

The kids headed out with their jackets and caps on. Helen made tomato bisque soup earlier and was warming up a bowl for her husband. As she entered the room to check on him, he was snoring, sound asleep. She gently closed the door and returned to the table to continue figuring out her crossword puzzle. It proved difficult for her to concentrate without thinking about how she enjoyed Cane and talking to him. His Southern accent and mannerism were indicative of how his parents raised him well. But all of these outstanding attributes were overshadowed once more by the fact that he was dead and that she didn't properly say good-bye.

Last night, after tempers settled, Cane's intensive gaze at her with those deep blue eyes was as though he was pleading for her to embrace him once more, almost childlike. She thought, should he have had slight feminine qualities or behaved differently around the kids? Was he purposely hiding his sexual orientation? Something wasn't adding up. She sadly remembered not being able to have eye contact with him when she said good night—an irrefutable moment in time never to be recaptured again.

Did Cane not tell us he was gay out of respect for us? Did he suspect the outcome he ultimately received? Our determination to not be intrusive may have been a missed opportunity for Cane to share what was going on with him. God, did we blow it? He respected our household, but that didn't prevent Dan from seizing the incriminatory moment. His informed statement was nothing less than taunting, which I still don't understand. How in God's name did we, moments away from an enjoyable perfect evening with newfound friends, erupt into a calamitous parting among strangers within seconds?

GUARDING REPUTATIONS

It was now eleven o'clock in the evening. Pastor Haugen's nap turned into a six-hour rest. Helen and the kids had eaten several hours earlier. Everyone was asleep, and she was watching a night show. Anders appeared from the bedroom and was smiling and yawning.

"Hey, Helen. I feel a hundred times better."

"All you needed was some shutdown time. I checked in on you, and once I heard the hard snoring."

"I've been up a little while praying. I sat on the edge of the bed, hoping everything that had happened was just a bad, bad dream."

"Real as can be. Anders, we are going to get through all of this. We always do."

"Yes, but these set of circumstances are like nothing we've experienced before. And I have to say this, God stopped Dan's truck in front of our house, and we drove up at the exact time intended. I'm telling you, God stalled that truck. Regardless of how the evening played out, it was all in God's plan."

"Something is off about this entire situation, I can feel it. It makes you want to ask, now what?"

"Helen, your instincts are on point."

"The kids waited up for you, but I persuaded them to go to bed."

"It's actually better we talk about everything first without them. What did you cook for dinner?"

"Pot roast, yams, and I saved you a large piece of Gilda's German chocolate cake before it was completely devoured."

"I'm starving."

"Take your time and eat first, and then we'll talk over a fresh cup of coffee."

"Sounds like a plan."

Pastor Anders was at a crucial impasse as a husband, father, and leader. His future decisions could either create an opportunity for God's greatness or damage his credibility. He reminded himself of the mountain story his father told him when he decided to leave the Lutheran church and begin a new work. "On our journeys, there are great mountains we need to climb in order to get to the other side. All we are able to see is what our human eyes can behold. Sometimes we are fearful of what lies ahead, but fear must always be left behind—it's of no use. God knows the traveler, the journey, and the obstacle. He created them all. Trust His mapped-out plan even if it doesn't make sense. He will never leave or forsake you."

"Helen, I love you!"

"I love you too. So what is our crisis?"

"I can't get too much pass now, can I?"

"Not too much. So what's going on?"

Helen poured them both a cup of coffee, and she sat down to listen.

"Let me begin with Cane. His name was Jeffrey Cane Peters, and he dropped Jeffrey when he moved out here. He was engaged to a woman—not a man—and during his bachelor party, he became intoxicated and somehow found himself in a compromising situation involving another man. Somehow, photos instantaneously appeared on social media, and the wedding was called off. His reputation was ruined, and he ardently denied ever being involved with another man. Not being able to recover from losing the love of his life, family embarrassment, and in a dark place, he left Kentucky for San Francisco about ten months ago."

"Oh my God, he was engaged to a woman, not a man?"

"That's right. Dan was dining at one of his favorite restaurants in Sausalito, and Cane was having it out with some guy—his roommate, I'm guessing—and was on the verge of being homeless. Dan overheard, felt sorry for him, and offered him a place to stay and a way to earn money. Dan was a very wealthy man—a millionaire, as a matter of fact. He was dying and needed a personal assistant."

"Dan was dying?"

He nodded.

"He had multiple sclerosis, AIDS, and he was unquestionably gay. He wanted some quiet time to finalize business matters, get his house in order, and most likely enjoy his last stay here in Tahoe. Do I now have your attention?"

"Wait one minute, let's get back to Cane. Cane lost everything and came out here, right?"

"Uh-huh."

"Were those photos real, you think?"

"Why are you asking about photos?"

"Anders, something isn't jiving here. Was he dating women and men?"

"Honey, I don't know the answer to that. At first, I admit I believed Dan when he said the both of them were gay, but Cane… now I'm not so sure. Even Nate, the attorney, had doubts."

"No, Anders. That young man may have become entangled in some weird situation, true, but it's not adding up. Maybe he was gay and decided it wasn't for him. Do you believe Dan was holding something over him? Why in God's name didn't he defend himself with us when he had the opportunity? We all picked up on him being agitated when Dan said they were gay. Why didn't he say something? Why didn't Cane defend himself?"

Helen began to cry, and she placed her hand over her mouth.

"Babe, please don't get yourself upset," he said, reaching over and patting her on the back. "He was such a caring and loveable young man. Did we blow it? I saw it in his eyes. The humiliation was in his eyes, and he needed us."

"Helen, Cane was broken on the inside, and none of us would have known it until Dan threw him under the bus. He left his support system back in Kentucky, and he was more than likely hanging on by a thread."

"What are you not telling me? His will to fight was gone. How do you know?"

"All I'm saying is that the opportunity presented itself, and he folded. Anyone else would have taken full advantage to defend their name. Cane seemed to care more about what Dan thought of him, not us."

"I'm telling you he had humiliation in his eyes. Stay with me on this one…I've got it."

"Now what are you talking about?"

"Listen, Dan, being gay, eventually figured out Cane wasn't gay, but Dan wanted Cane to believe he didn't know. Talk about serious mind games. As the kids would say, Dan busted him out, and he was caught completely off guard. It was a situation of 'darn if you do or darn if you don't.'"

"Helen!"

"I believe it's the truth. He would have had to call Dan an outright liar, which meant siding with us against him, and who knows what dirty laundry Dan would have hung out. Poor Cane, he figured that calculated risk wasn't in his favor," Helen said in an upsetting voice.

"I'm going to tell you what I've concluded and what gives me peace. We reacted based on what was presented, and I don't believe we would have done much differently. So at the end of the day, we pray, learn from the situation, and move on. I've decided if or when his parents agree to join us for dinner, we will omit the drama and focus on dinner, the fun selfies, and the plans he made to go skiing with us. It is a given, the Peters have had a difficult time being separated from their son as it is, and Nate said they hadn't communicated since he left Kentucky. At the very least, we will leave them with an impression that not only Cane was proud of his family, but that they too should be proud of him. I'm going to ask Peter to print out the selfies on nice photo paper."

"Sarah and me will go down to one of the shops and pick up a couple of nice picture frames." Helen continued to tear up and repeatedly covered her mouth in fear of a wail.

"Let's bless the Peters with peace and some comfort. And this will help all of us to heal. No need to leave heartbreaking memories with them. I had this exact conversation with Nate yesterday and quoted Proverbs chapter fifteen, verse thirty, 'Light in a messenger's eyes brings light to the heart, and good news gives health to the bones.'"

"Come on, Helen. Let's go to bed. The rest of what I want to tell you can wait until morning."

Anders and Helen cleaned the kitchen and retired for the evening.

The next morning at six o'clock…

After their morning prayer, Pastor Haugen and Helen decided to have coffee early and discuss his meeting with Nate.

"Dan was a millionaire, and he had no living relatives, so his estate has been divided among his friends and projects. He was disinherited for many years when he told his parents he was gay during college spring break, but it was reinstated when the last known relative passed away. He missed his mother dearly during this separation, and he needed her."

Pastor Haugen explained detail after detail of Dan's Aunt Sovenia, Nate, and a dying man's last wish for the Luccia House.

"If you weren't my husband that I've known for over twenty years, I'd believe you made all of this up. Oh my Lord!"

"Yes, it is over-the-top!"

"That too is an understatement."

"I think we need to follow our plans with the Peters and end it there. Need I remind you of our October Bible classes on homosexuality and the church?"

"No."

In October, Pastor Haugen offered a series of classes on homosexuality called The New Gender Plan, also referred to as the NGP. He taught God's gender plan is and will always be perfect; it was his original master piece. When you alter His gender plan, there are consequences. These NGPs have an appearance of right due to self-will, but are still an abomination to God. Gays are determined to undermine and prove they are more powerful than God by establishing and participating in the NGP. Homosexuality has been in existence since recorded biblical times, but what's new are the contemporary legalities.

"Listen to me, Anders. Let someone else take on the responsibility of the Luccia House. How are you going to spearhead a home for aging gays? Who cares if it's forty-four million or four hundred forty million? We know it's not about the money. Oh, no. Please don't tell me that you are considering taking this on? No way."

"I've been praying consistently, and I have to tell you my spirit is moving in another direction."

"What direction? Anders, don't even consider it. Please."

"God is taking me in another direction, and without saying, it does not waver from my position on homosexuality."

"Okay, where is all this going? I don't like the sound of this."

"Will you just listen to me for a minute? All our lives, this family has been dedicated to helping feed the underprivileged, the mission fields, and the list goes on. All of these projects were in our comfort zone. Our comfort zone, Helen. People and places we chose and preferred to be a part of. Suppose now, just suppose, God has given us an assignment we don't prefer to do. He certainly would not ask us to do anything that causes us to sin. Never. That's not the God we worship or believe in. I'm telling you, while I was meditating, Jonah came to my mind over and over. It was God speaking to me."

Helen was silent. She began to fold kitchen towels as her husband awaited a response.

"Honey, don't you see? It's all coming together! The Rover breaking down, their death, and me arriving literally minutes prior to Dan dying. No coincidence here. Does it make sense? Absolutely not. We simply follow God as we've always done. This family has witnessed too many times God's way of doing things. Remember our beautiful Sarah when she left us, and, God bless, he returned her spirit back to us? Remember?"

"Anders! Why are you asking me if I remember? How many times have I looked at her and cringed just thinking how we would have missed out on our angel?"

Helen was in labor over fourteen hours with Sarah and required an emergency TJian. After the delivery, there was no heartbeat, and Sarah was pronounced dead. Helen later told Anders that when she initially heard the news, she asked God why He would take her baby girl. She immediately reflected on months prior—going into debt purchasing a vehicle for a family member who desperately needed a car and Anders donating bone marrow—they had given so much! But the Spirit restored her faith, and she surrendered to the grim reality.

> For by grace are ye saved through faith; and that not of yourselves: it is the gift of God, Not of works, lest any man should boast. (Eph. 2:8–9)

The moment the scripture crossed her heart, a surreal spirit rested on her soul, and Sarah's heart miraculously began to beat. To this day, it was still difficult for Helen to explain other than it was God's testing of her faith. She had repeated this testimony hundreds of times to those who needed a deeper understanding of how everyone had fears and that fear must be brought under control.

For God hath not given us the spirit of fear; but of power, and of love, and of a sound mind. (2 Tim. 1:7)

"Have you ever known me not to support you with anything? Never. This is no exception. I remember when I first met you, you were mature and pragmatic, and that won me over. So, Anders, if your spirit is compelling you to go in this direction, I don't want to be a stumbling block or cause you to go against the will of God. Not me. And Jonah?"

"Yes. Jonah was called by God, but he wanted to do things his way. He thought he had a better plan than God Almighty."

"Before you make a final decision, give yourself a couple of days and please wait before you share this with the kids and have some sort of plan. Please! Andrew, Peter, and Sarah are all biblically astute and can stand their own ground. This is how we've raised them. Plan to expect the unexpected from them. Keep in mind, homosexuals are not just gays and lesbians."

"I know all of this."

"Let me finish. There are same-sex marriage issues, transgenders and people who are openly promoting freedom to experience any gender. It's dangerously layered in comparison from the time when we were growing up. Aging gays may include all of this and more. Yes, I'm preaching to the choir, but hear me out now on my soapbox. Anyone can experience being alone, not just gays. However, those aging gays made a conscious decision to engage in that lifestyle early on, I'm guessing. So, Anders, I leave you with this. As long as it's God's plan, not yours, to God be the glory. Tread carefully. I will stand by you."

Pastor Anders looked at Helen with an emotionally assuring contentment. Now his confidence was strengthened.

"Thank you. I think a fire would be nice right about now."

She smiled. Pastor Haugen took his jacket off the coat rack near the back door and headed out to the side of the house for firewood. TJ began to bark and scratch the door.

"TJ. TJ." Helen sang.

The door opened, and TJ dashed to the table.

"Morning, Mom," said Andrew.

"Good morning. I hope everyone wakes up famished. I'm in the mood to cook a hungry jack breakfast, potatoes and all. Hello, my TJ. Hello, boooy!"

"I'm ready. I heard Dad getting wood."

TJ was barking and scratching the back door, and Andrew opened it.

"It was apparent the kids genuinely liked those two. I believe they were disappointed with Cane. Maybe disappointed isn't the best way to describe their reaction, but they were connecting with him and enjoying his company. All three of them were taken aback when they were told he died. Don't you agree?"

"You're absolutely right."

"I don't understand why you need to include them with this decision. Just say emphatically no to the attorney, and let's move on from this. It's your decision. Are you that unsure about things?"

At the morning walk…

After breakfast, the Haugens headed out for an early family walk and meeting. They located a small bluff about one half a mile away from their home. The five Haugens formed a circle and held hands, and Pastor Haugen went into prayer.

"Oh, merciful heavenly Father, thank you for blessing us to see another one of your glorious days. Please be with me and my family at this time as we discuss past and future events. May we share our thoughts in love and in a manner that is not only pleasing in your sight, but also aligns with your precious Word. Father, we ask that you give traveling grace to the Peters family as they travel here to return their son, Cane, back to Kentucky. Please give comfort to their grieving spirits at this time. Also, comfort the grieving dear friends of Dan Piattoni and provide them with traveling grace to return him home to his final resting place. May all find comfort in the memories of Cane and Dan. It is in Jesus Christ our Lord's name we pray, let us all say, Amen."

All said amen.

"Get comfortable. Find a spot."

Sarah huddled with her mom on a broken tree, while Peter and Andrew stood.

"No special reason for bringing everyone out here, just wanted to do something different. As a pastor, husband, and your father, it is my responsibility to manage a godly life for those under my watchful eye. This is a commandment by the Almighty. I can say with confidence that your mother and I feel we've done a good job in part because we've got great kids. We chose to live in Elk Grove—it's a pretty decent suburb with good neighbors I might add, and I'm equally as proud of our congregation. There are growing families, and we're all striving for the same cause—the cause of Christ. Every day of all of your lives, Helen and I have prayed for you, mainly because we love you and we realize that as a pastor's kids, it makes you a prime target. Let me repeat myself, it makes you a prime target being a pastor's kids. People hold you to a higher, sometimes an unrealistic, standard, and the enemy does not waste any time trying to ensnare you.

"Also, as realist, we know that eventually the three of you will one day leave us and begin living your own lives, as you should. Until that time, we make it a point to protect and prepare you as much as possible. Once you strike out on your own, you will endure all of life's challenges—good and not so good alike. However, in life as parents, you get a curveball from time to time, and your kids are exposed to situations you wish happened when they are adults and more mature to handle. Experience is quite different from textbook or Bible class, if you will. It has those unexpected nuisances. Trust me, kids, when I say your mother and I are not that naïve when it comes to your many classmates beliefs that are different from one end of the spectrum to the other, not by a long shot. Is everyone with me?"

Pastor Haugen looked at his kids one by one to receive their acknowledgment.

"What we experienced as a family a couple of days ago, that curveball I wish would have come around a few years out, but it is what it is. Case in point, I made a decision to assist Dan and Cane when they were in trouble. I want all of you to know that if I had to do it all over again, I would have done the same. Yesterday, I learned more about them and how their deaths impacted the loved ones left behind. Let's start with Cane. His real name was Jeffrey Cane Peters. Less than a year ago, he moved to San Francisco and dropped Jeffrey and went by Cane. His parents and a twin sister, Jennifer, will be here today, if they already haven't arrived. His parents are beyond devastated losing their only son. When he was here sharing his stories of Kentucky, it was all true. However, he left out some incidents, which is understandable, but that was his prerogative, and this is how we plan to keep it. By this, I mean everything prior to Dan telling us they were gay is fine to share. Just for the record, your mom and I didn't really buy into him being gay."

"I knew it!" shouted Andrew. "I told you, Pete."

"Ah, man," said Peter.

"Let's not digress, let me finish. There'll be plenty of time for that. He's gone, and the truth went with him. It serves no purpose to harp onto or go into a discussion about Cane's sexual orientation, or why Dan shared that information."

Andrew and Peter started talking between themselves.

"Come on now, guys, let me finish what I need to say. He was engaged to be married to a young lady in Kentucky, and the night before their wedding at a bachelor party, Cane was intoxicated and found himself in an embarrassing and compromising situation with another man. Today it does not matter. He's gone. Let's remember what he presented to us—nothing more, nothing less.

"There is one more thing. Dan's attorney, Nate, conveyed to his parents we are Christians, and I'm a pastor too! I've asked Cane's parents to contact me. Your mom and I decided to invite them to dinner. They need to know he spent the night here—minus the drama of course. It's enough they are grieving their son. This will give them a sense of peaceful closure, knowing he was among Christians before his death. If anything contrary arises, remember, it's not going to come from us. Am I making myself clear?"

Andrew responded, "Not a problem, Dad."

He looked at Sarah.

"Sure."

"Peter?"

"No problem."

"God forbid, if anything were to happen to any one of you, your mom and I would want to know and appreciate how you spent your last moments of life. I'll let you in on something else. Cane and his parents had not spoken one word between them since leaving Kentucky after the incident, so to hear of his passing is heartwrenching. The Haugens will bless the Peters with pleasantries of how he loved and spoke highly of his family, congregation, and his infectious laugh. Peter, I want you to print out all the pictures, especially the selfies, on a good photo paper. You and Andrew pick out a couple of nice ones. Helen and Sarah will go to one of the shops and buy nice picture frames for them.

"While I'm on the subject. Andrew, Peter, and Sarah, it is a given that in all probability you will do or say something that will hurt us or we will be strongly at odds. Your mom and I may get angry as heck and say or do something you don't agree with, but never ever allow whatever it is to cause either of you to not communicate with us. We love you too much, and we will always be there for each of you, and whatever it is, we will work through it by God's grace. Understand, Andrew?"

"Yes."

"Understand, Peter?"

"I'm with you."

"Baby girl?"

"Sure thing, Mom and Dad."

Helen took a tissue from her pocket and wiped away tears. Sarah kissed her on the cheek.

"Life is difficult, and that's why support systems are crucial. You have one with us and the congregation. The enemy is waiting for a wedge, and he doesn't miss any opportunities. Just keep this in mind. Your mom is sitting here tearing up because she's a mother, and I'm a pastor and a father, like Cane's parents, and the idea of one of you becoming isolated and something terrible happening to you during this time is simply inconceivable. Cane and his parents are the perfect example of believing time is always on your side."

"The Haugens will not be problem free. That isn't realistic in a fallen world. What is realistic is being able to work through whatever it is," chimed in Helen.

"We are not here to blame his parents or Cane, but rather the consequences. This is what I know about Dan."

"Sorry, dad, you've both made your point, and we get it. Andrew and I were talking last night and could not figure out why Mr. Piattoni waited until the last minute to tell us they were gay."

Pastor Haugen and Helen locked eyes.

"Yeah, Mom. Cane switched gears completely when Mr. Piattoni told us. It's like he didn't want us to know that and was ticked off at him. Then when dad and Mr. Piattoni went back and forth, he had nothing more to say," said Peter.

"He looked embarrassed," Andrew added.

"As your father said earlier, they're both gone, and there's only room for speculation now, that's all."

"Now for Daniel Piattoni. He was a multimillionaire who was, without a doubt, gay and an atheist. He had no children or other living relatives. However, he had very close friends who loved him as a brother. He's well-known in San Francisco for helping underprivileged musically inclined children and other social causes. I spoke to him before he passed away. He wanted me to tell everyone he was sorry for not being a better guest and was happy to have known us."

"Ahhh, Dad, really?" asked Sarah.

"Dan was terminally ill. He shared with us that he had been under the weather. In fact, he had multiple sclerosis, AIDS, and was not expected to live much longer. He was here to finalize some business and get his house in order."

"Ah, man, that's sad!" said Peter.

"Dad, do you regret letting them borrow our truck?" asked Sarah.

"Not at all. It was in God's plan. Joe Martin took a look at the Range Rover, and there was absolutely nothing wrong with it."

"Spooky! Freaky! When Cane and I went back down for the duffel bag, I looked under the hood while he attempted to see if it would turn over, and nothing," Andrew added.

"To move this discussion in another direction, what blessing came out of all of this? I'll start. Cane's parents will receive pictures of him laughing and having a good time. Helen?"

"As a family, we've seen firsthand what devastating consequences can occur when you don't communicate, and we've agreed never to allow this to happen to the Haugens."

"Sarah."

"I remember Mr. Piattoni taking one picture, and we should make copies too with a frame and give it to his best friend."

"Beautiful. Peter, your turn."

"I know I'm the stubborn one, so I'm thankful God showed me how too much stubbornness can ruin your life and others who love you."

"Can I get that in writing?" Andrew said sarcastically.

"All right, Andrew, don't let me get on you, Mr. Know-It-All. What's your takeaway?"

"Appreciating my family more after seeing what it's like to not have one."

Andrew got hit in the face with a snowpack from Peter, and TJ jumped on him.

"That's my signature in writing."

"What, am I an easy target? You too, TJ. Where's the loyalty?"

"Anders, I'm missing that warm fire right about now."

"Let's go, Mom. I'm with you."

"I'm with you too! Andrew and Peter, you staying or coming?"

"Staying!"

"Yeah, me too!"

"Got your cell?" asked Pastor Haugen.

"I've got mine," Peter replied.

Andrew waved his. He and Peter played fetch with TJ and continued to dodge snowballs at each other. Pastor Haugen, Helen, and Sarah headed back to their home and indulged in Helen's hot chocolate. Pastor Haugen kept his word to his wife and did not discuss the Luccia House with the kids until he had a concise biblical explanation for any decision. As suggested, Helen and Sarah went shopping and located two appropriate frames for both Cane and Dan.

On Wednesday evening…

At 6:20, Pastor Haugen received a call from Nate. Pastor Charles Peters, his wife Allison, and daughter Jennifer arrived earlier in the day. Cane's body would be released in the morning, and the Peters were scheduled to leave tomorrow afternoon from Tahoe to return to San Francisco. They accepted his invitation to meet him and his family, but midmorning was their only time available, and it would be brief. Nate gave him Pastor Peters's cell phone number, and he called to confirm and provide the address. They planned to arrive at ten in the morning.

On Thursday morning...

The Haugens were seated at the table having breakfast. Pastor Haugen, with his many years of experience dealing with grieving families, realized this was a new paradigm—strangers, and yet not so strangers. He reinforced the importance of remaining encouraging and to respect any boundaries the Peters established in their conversations. Intrusiveness is off-limits.

"Dad, it seems as though we are getting slammed at one time. Nonstop with one crazy thing after the other," Andrew commented.

"I know, son. Remember, the best made plans can change."

"Keep in mind, Andrew, this is the result of a tragic car accident and the people it affected. When people lose loved ones out of their area, someone has to take charge and be responsible for all the arrangements. In this case, it's Cane's entire immediate family," said Helen.

"Mom, I still can't believe they're gone. It's so sad," added Sarah.

"Let's finish up. We need to be presentable and not rushed when they arrive. I think I'll put out the banana nut bread I made this morning just in case."

Helen went to the laundry area to sort out clothes for washing, while the kids all pitched in and cleaned the kitchen. Pastor Haugen went upstairs to the deck and sat.

At nine forty-five, an SUV slowly pulled up in the drive; it was the Peters. The driver, Pastor Peters, walked over, opened the passenger door, and assisted his wife Allison and daughter Jennifer. Momentarily pausing and taking in the view, Mrs. Peter said something, and then they walked up to the steps, recognizing the dated sign, "Welcome to Blue Castle."

"That's cute. It's probably something one of the kids painted when they were young," said Jennifer.

Mrs. Peters stopped.

"You okay, honey? You don't have to do this. I can tell them you aren't up to this," asked Pastor Peters.

"No, that would be rude. We're here now. Let's just get this over with."

He held her arm and continued. Pastor Haugen opened the door and greeted them as Mrs. Peters led. This Southern family exuded culture and refinement. She was petite, strikingly attractive with shoulder-length blond hair. She was wearing a black pee coat, a black-and-beige wrap, ankle-length boots, and black gloves. Cane strongly resembled his mother. His twin, Jennifer, was tall like her brother with athletic build and long-flowing chestnut-brown hair. Her green wool coat was knee-length, with black boots exposing only a portion of her legs. Pastor Peters was six feet, three inches tall with a slender build. He was sporting a hat and was sharply dressed from head to toe in all black.

"Good morning. I'm Anders. Thank you for stopping by."

Pastor Peters removed his hat. "Good morning, and we appreciate your invite. I'm Charles, and this is my wife, Allison, and our daughter, Jennifer."

"This is Helen, my oldest, Andrew, and then Peter and Sarah. Oh, and TJ."

"Hello."

"Hello."

"Please have a seat. May I offer you tea, coffee, or water?" asked Helen.

"No, thank you."

"No, thank you."

"First of all, we would like to say we are truly, truly sorry for your loss. Cane was a really polite and nice young man."

"Cane?" asked Pastor Peters as he looked at Allison.

"I'm sorry, did I say something wrong?" asked Pastor Haugen.

"His name is Jeffrey Cane." Then he paused. "His name was Jeffrey Cane, and I find it odd he was using his middle name," added Pastor Peters.

"Charles, young people often change their names when they relocate or start over. It's natural," said Pastor Haugen.

"It's just odd hearing it like that. Nothing more."

"Mr. Horowitz told me Jeffrey was on his way up here with his employer when his SUV stalled, and you and your family was kind to help them and offer a temporary place to stay. For that, we are grateful."

"While they were waiting for road service that never showed, he played the PS4 with Andrew and Peter. They ate dinner with us and had a nice time," said Helen. "I know you've probably heard this all your life, but Jeffrey was your splitting image. My goodness," she also added.

"Sure does," said Peter.

"We were planning to go skiing and snowboarding," Andrew said.

"All of my kids are involved in youth ministries, and Jeffrey told us about your congregation and the youth ministries. Everyone immediately seemed to connect. And that infectious laugh of his…," said Pastor Haugen.

"You can say that again, Dad!" Sarah commented.

Allison let out a deep sigh and appeared heartbroken. Helen looked at Sarah and pointed to the gift bag. She went to the kitchen table and handed Mrs. Peters a green and blue festive gift bag with white and gold tissue paper.

"A gift?"

"Oh, yes. We have put something very special together for you and your family. I hope you will enjoy it," said Helen.

"Mrs. Peters, this is our gift from the Haugens to the Peters family," said Sarah.

"Thank you."

"Cane—I mean, Jeffrey—was so nice," Sarah added.

"That's okay," Jennifer responded.

Mrs. Peters took her time and gently removed the items. There were two framed photos of Jeffrey—one an outlandish selfie with the Haugenbunch and the other standing alone by the fireplace. Pastor Peters looked over. She held the two frames of her deceased son, Jeffrey, and seemingly lost her balance as she sat on the sofa beside her husband and daughter. Then suddenly, she inhaled a deep breath and unleashed a loud moan, which was followed by a scream. The entire household was in disbelief and became unnerved.

"Jeffrey! My Jeffrey! Oh, God!"

"Sarah, get me a cold wet towel now. Andrew, go get a pillow from my bedroom. Please, now."

Sarah almost tripped but then recomposed herself and rushed to the linen closet. She grabbed a wash towel and then went to the kitchen sink. Andrew hurried with the pillow. Everyone in the room was now teary. Pastor Peters held his wife.

"I'm sorry, everyone, but I believe it's best we leave now. This trip has proven to be too much for us all."

Helen patted Jennifer on the back and motioned to let her sit by Allison. As Jennifer stood, her mother cried aloud and screamed again. This time, Helen held Allison.

"Scream! Let it out! Scream!"

Pastor Peters was flushed. "Oh, Allison. She's been holding up so well."

Jennifer also cried. "Mom!"

"Anders, please show Pastor Peters the grounds, and, kids, you take Jennifer to the lake. Please, now," Helen said in a calm yet crackling commanding voice.

"She will be just fine. Please, Jennifer!"

"No, I'd rather stay here with my mom."

"Please. It will be okay."

"Come on, Jen. Let's do as she suggests."

"Mom, I don't want to leave. Will you be all right?"

Her mother didn't respond. She just stared, crying. Sarah handed her mother the cold wet towel. Jennifer and the kids left the home one by one. Pastor Peters walked over to his wife, rubbed her back, and left with Pastor Haugen. Helen placed the pillow on the sofa, and Allsion lay back.

"Cry, Allison. Let it all out. Don't be ashamed to scream. Jeffrey was your son. You gave him life."

Allison cried profusely. "Jeff! My Jeff! Dear God, I miss you. I'm so sorry."

"Say it again, Allison."

"I miss you, Jeff, and I'm so sorry."

Helen soothingly rubbed her forehead with the towel. She pushed back Helen's hand and said, "I hadn't spoken to him in almost a year. What parent who loves their child does that? Who?"

Helen listened attentively.

"God, forgive me for being such a terrible parent. Who treats their baby like that? Jeff, I'm so sorry."

"How was everything before you stop communicating?"

"Perfect."

"Listen to me, Allison, and listen good. You aren't a terrible parent because of a misunderstanding. People will disagree, be right and wrong. We're flawed that way. No one but God knows when you will be able to laugh and smile about your memories with Jeffrey, but you will. When he was here a couple of days ago, with that infectious laugh, he spoke so highly of you and your husband. No, I take that back—he literally bragged. Does that sound like someone who was angry or unforgiving to his mother? No. When I first met him, I said to myself, this young man is so well-mannered and was raised properly. You and your husband did that."

"Thank you."

"No, don't thank me. Thank God. Our husbands are pastors, and God wanted to make sure your prayers were answered. Oh, I know without question you were praying for him every day. God's miracle was to allow Jeffrey to spend his last hours among other Christians and share that firsthand with his family, so I'm thankful to God for this opportunity."

"Helen, yesterday Jen woke up and was distressed, almost horrified, and said something is wrong. I asked her what she meant something was wrong, and she said, 'Mom, we need to get in touch with Jeff. I believe he's in a lot of trouble.' Then I started crying. That's when she said that she had a bad feeling."

Allison pointed to her heart. "I know her, she knew, but didn't say it. Dear God, we have such high hopes for our children, and when they disappoint us, we can be unreasonable. I was unreasonable. No, our family was unreasonable, and we drove him away."

She wept loudly. Helen got on her knees and continued to comfort.

"After Sarah was born, her heart stopped beating, and she was pronounced dead."

Allison looked in disbelief.

"In that moment, it was all about me, me, me and how I was feeling. I'm certain if someone walked up to me and said it was God's will, I would have probably slapped them—oh, yes, I'm not kidding. I would have told them to get out of my presence."

She was once again astounded at Helen's comments.

"I had to ask God Almighty the creator for forgiveness. Why? Because I felt I knew what was best and that taking her life wasn't it. After all, I'm Helen, and what does God know about my life, what I need, and, furthermore, what was best for Sarah? I was speaking from an indignant and emotional frame of mind. Well, guess again, we all do. Jeffrey is present with the Lord, and this incident did not take God by surprise—only you and your loved ones. This was his appointed time to leave here. Did you grasp what I said? His appointed time. Find comfort in knowing he spoke of his mother in love rather than resentment. Jeffrey will be patiently waiting for you on the other side. If he could speak to you now, I believe he'd say, 'I love you, but more importantly, thank you, Mother.'"

"Why would Jeffrey say thank you?"

"Because you loved him, and that's what sustained him during your absence. Love."

"Thank you, Helen."

"No, don't thank me. Thank God alone. You will continue to cry, be angry, don't want to be bothered, and miss him something awful, but with God's grace, He will grant you mercy and peace."

Allison and Helen hugged as though they'd been friends for a lifetime.

"Would you like a fresh cup of tea or coffee?"

"I'll take the tea."

"Great. You can sit here, or you'll miss a spectacular view that Jeffrey himself enjoyed. There's a bathroom to the left if you'd like to freshen up a bit as well."

Allison barely cracked a smile and chose to freshen up. Helen set out fresh banana nut bread and honey while Allison steeped the tea. Helen and Allison then sat quietly, admiring the majestic Sierra Mountains.

"I want to leave you with this, Allison, for all its worth. When the services are over and you've laid your son to rest, you will set the tone for the grieving and healing of your family and loved ones. Regardless of your load, they will depend on you. Cry, say a few choice words. Don't let too many people hear about the latter, but survive with God's wonderful and powerful grace. Also, water has such a healing and cleansing effect on me, and maybe for you too. Sooner rather than later, you and your family should take an unplanned trip to the lake or ocean, even if it is the winter. Go for a few days and be off-limits to the norm of things. Just a thought to pass on."

"We're so blessed and thankful to God Jeffrey became acquainted with you all. It was good for him, even if it was so brief. As you said, it was a miracle, and I will never forget all of this as long as I live."

"Allison, if the tables were turned, I know you would do the same for my children."

"I would."

"I know."

The impeccable timing of God allowed for, one, the intimate process of grief to begin and, two, the God-given gift to exhort. Pastor Haugen decided both families should tour the grounds and lake together when they left. Jennifer walked over to her mother, stroked her back, and smiled.

"You okay, Mom?"

"Yes, Jen!" Allsion said. Then she turned to her husband. "Honey, it's beautiful up here. Helen told me Jeffrey enjoyed this exact view. Here, take a look and see what he found so fascinating."

The apprehensiveness Pastor Peters felt in dealing with his previously hysterical wife was replaced with a delightful relieved expression accompanied by restrained tears as he joined her by the oversized bay windows.

"Kentucky has some breathtaking places. I must say South Lake Tahoe is incredible," said Pastor Peters.

"Charles, I know we are pressed for time. I'd like to stay a little longer so we can remember all of this. Jen, you okay with that?"

"Sure, Mom. It's up to you."

"If that's what you want, Allison, we can spare at least another half an hour," Pastor Peters added.

"This is great," Pastor Haugen added.

Within a span of forty-five minutes, the Haugens, with a determination to reveal their encounter with Jeffrey, was joined by the Peters in sharing his childhood crazy moments, the adventures of his young adult life, and the two ministry trips to Africa and Mexico.

Mr. Jeffrey Cane Peters momentarily lost his way, but by God's grace, compassionate strangers, a beloved family, guided his true spirit into their memories forever.

Both the Haugens and Peterses agreed to remain in touch.

The Jonah Syndrome

On Friday morning…

Pastor Haugen and Helen found themselves again engaged in an intense conversation about days past, particularly the Peterses and the Luccia House. The entire household was emotionally exhausted from the original argument, the accident, and the meeting with the grieving Peterses.

"Helen, we are being tested like never before. Not so much individually, but more collectively as a family. I'm starting to sound like one of the kids now. This vacation feels more like a mystery marathon. I should be relaxed, and yet I'm on edge. I know I've said it twice, but I have to hand it to you for quick thinking in handling Mrs. Peters. She was about to lose it, and you used that Helen touch and reeled her back in. Thank God."

"You are right. Thank God—and He alone, not by my might. That family has a long road ahead, and they will be all right. I'm sure of it. Now what about the Luccia obstacle?"

"I guess you know by now I've decided to take this on?"

"Oh, yeah."

"Can you believe it? Here I am, about to get involved with a forty-four-million-dollar project and with trepidation sharing it with the kids and the world. What's wrong with that picture?"

"It's not what's wrong with that picture, but it's what's wrong with people."

"When Nate initially spoke to me about this undertaking, he added the person involved is compensated with five percent of that—half in the beginning and the balance when it is completed."

"I was waiting for you to tell me, Anders. I knew an amount was attached somewhere. When he needed to get your attention, did you really think an experienced attorney would not bait you with a five-percent carrot? Of course, you'd have to be compensated."

"Really, honey?"

"Yes. That's a nice chunk of change, and you were going to share this information when?"

"Kids' college fund, youth ministries, and our mission projects. This has me thinking about our own Christian senior facility outside of Elk Grove. Our baby boomers, who are not necessarily prepared for retirement, would be blessed with this kind of affordable housing project. Other congregations around the country are doing the same thing, so this isn't really something new."

"Honey, let's get the horse out the gate first, even though he's pulling a gold chariot."

"Just thinking aloud."

"Now since we skirted through the surface conversation, is the argument with Dan bothering you at all?"

"Helen, I love you. Does it show?"

"Not at all. You're human, and you're my husband."

"It's one of those things you, perhaps, never get fully past. I seem to be managing the thoughts well…getting there."

"Okay, preaching to the preacher, but it was God's divine destiny. I've been thinking too. That night when you and Dan were talking, I overheard you sharing proudly about our ministries, and that may have sparked him to thinking you would be the perfect fit for the Luccia House. I believe had he not passed away, he would have approached you. Just a thought here."

"I never took that into account."

Helen was requiring reassurance that any form of remorse was not the driving force with him proceeding with this unusual and controversial undertaking. The kids soon would be up for breakfast, and as their agreed-upon marriage covenant, it was critical to maintain a cohesive front, regardless of their differences. Helen had prepared homemade yeast biscuits and covered them with a cloth.

"Helen, I'm going to tell the kids about the Luccia House during breakfast. I can tell you still have strong reservations, and that's okay. I'm going to try my best to present this as an acceptable project."

"Anders, I do hope so. For all our sakes, I don't want this project to be misunderstood or your intent taken out of context. You will need to somehow strike a delicate balance. I know I sound like a broken record, but again, what you decide, moving forward, is going to affect this entire family for the remainder of our lives. This has long-term effects. I played it out in my head, and there may be criticism from within the body. Are you ready?"

"I am."

"Are you going to tell the kids your plan, or do you plan to ask for their opinions?"

"A little of both. I only want to get a feel for where their heads are, that's all."

"Okay."

"I have a few of my own ideas I'd like to add to this project, keeping in mind that everyone is worthy to be saved."

"Like what?"

"Adding a sanctuary, if there isn't one."

"Well, I give you credit for being ambitious. I wonder how that's going to go over."

"I will walk away from the project if I am not able to, even when it appears there is no hope. That's the Great Commission. It's simple in word yet difficult oftentimes in task to accomplish."

"Good point, Pastor Haugen. Do what you have to do."

"Thank you, Sister Helen."

They laughed and chatted for a while until Sarah emerged.

"Morning!" Sarah yawned.

"Good morning!"

"Morning, baby girl."

"This vacation is exhausting. Am I the only one who feels like this?"

"Oh, yes, we've been busy, and there is, perhaps, more to come."

"Dad, it's taking the V out of vacation. We have one more day here and then it's New Year's Eve. I was thinking about Cane too. Even though we didn't know him well, I miss him. His Southern charm and accent. He was a nice guy."

"We will never forget those two, and I'm proud you are thinking about the positive side of things."

"Of course."

"An old cliché, and I will say it anyway. I can't wait for the New Year, new beginnings. It doesn't matter if we spend one day or one week as long as we are doing it together."

"Quality time here in the mountains," Helen added.

"I get your point. Uh-uh, here he comes. Hello, TJ!"

Andrew had barely opened the bedroom door, and TJ made a dash for Pastor Haugen.

"Dad, this vacation seems shorter. Today is Friday, and the week is zipping by."

"My goodness, Sarah just said the same. We've had people in and out, that's all. We are used to being alone."

"You mean major drama. When do we eat?"

"Not for another half an hour. My yeast biscuits have thirty more minutes to rise. What about juice or hot chocolate?"

"I'll take the juice," said Sarah.

"I'll take a large mug of chocolate. Oh, here comes Sleeping Beauty."

"Morning, everyone. Did I miss anything?"

"Morning, Peter. No breakfast for at least a half an hour until your mom's yeast biscuits finish rising. What do you want to drink? Juice or hot chocolate?"

"Juice."

"Helen, now is the perfect time, don't you think?"

"Go for it."

"Wow! What's going on now? This vacation will go down in history as being ridiculously dramatic," said Andrew.

"This is part two of our first discussion, so get your drinks and have a seat. When I went to the hospital to see Dan, Nate said he was actually holding on for me despite the fact all of his close friends were there. Dan was dying of AIDS and didn't have long to live. Yes, he had already prepared himself. His visit here to his home was intentional. He wanted to be there for the last time and finalize some business. Dan's mother, Luccia Piattoni, impacted his life tremendously. To the point that he wanted her remembered even after his death."

"Oh, poor Mr. Piattoni," said Sarah.

"Dan was working on a project called the Luccia House in honor of his mother, a place where aging gay people can live. He put forty-four million dollars aside for this project."

"Forty-four million? Aging gays?" asked Peter.

"Yes, forty-four million for an aging gay facility in Tiburon. This was to be his pride and joy project. Dan and Nate had a simple and ingenious plan in the event he had not appointed anyone to oversee the Luccia House, and he was on his deathbed. Dan would ask the unbeknownst person to give him both of his hands, he would kiss them, nod at Nate, and then Nate would reciprocate to seal the deal. Also, this gesture with its meaning is in his will. You are looking at the person Dan requested to take over the project."

"And you turned it down, right?" asked Peter.

"I told Nate I would get back with him, perhaps, next week."

"Which means you are giving it some thought," added Peter.

"Dad, you're going to walk away from this, right?" asked Andrew.

"Oh my goodness, Dad, almost forty-four million dollars!" shouted Sarah.

However, Peter responded sternly with his eyes and was silent. Helen took her husband's hand to show a parental solidarity.

"Dad, please walk away from this. You don't owe Dan anything. It was only a request. You are not obligated," said Andrew.

"Peter?"

"Dad, I'm with Andrew. Walk away! You have nothing to prove. Are you feeling guilty about loaning them the Tacoma and dying because of the accident? I hope not."

"No, son. My conscious is clear."

"Mom, I know you have something to say about this. So what do you think?" asked Andrew.

"To be perfectly honest, I wanted him to walk too. Oh, yes, I did. But Anders is wise and has been in prayer. I think this is an opportunity to help people. No, I know this is an opportunity to help people."

"Oh my God! Unbelievable! Unbelievable! Let someone else have the responsibility of this project. Do you realize what people will say? Please, Dad, don't agree to take this on," said Peter.

"Andrew, please! Is that all you're worried about? What people will say? You need to get over yourself! Dad, I know you and Mom will make the right decision, and whatever you decide, I'm with you," said Sarah.

"Sarah, you don't know what you're talking about. You don't get it. Dad, people will think we've taken sides with the gays. Even if you don't care what people say about you, think about us three. Think about it! They will run with this one. Talk about taking pot-shots," Andrew said sharply.

Peter stood and mused.

"Dad, this is too close to the fire, and we all may get burned for it. Are you trying to prove something? I am emphatically opposed to this. In the youth ministry, we passionately advocate how homosexuality is wrong, and now we're going to be part of some sort of final resting place. The line has to be drawn. If not this, then what's next? Why in God's name did we spend almost the entire month of October teaching a series on the new gender plan?" Peter added angrily.

"Okay, are you all done? Have a seat, Peter."

In disgust, Andrew said, "Dad, I have one more thing to say. I pray that you've considered the short- and long-term ramifications. And what about our congregation? I just don't get it. I know you said your conscious is clear, but guilt maybe is the cloak and dagger here. Oh, last I checked, homosexuality includes same-sex marriages and transgenders too. Let them help their own. Dang."

With an outburst, Sarah said, "Oh my God!"

"That's enough, you two!" Pastor Haugen said as he stood and walked to the window, peering out.

"Haugenbunch, listen. Remember the story of Jonah? Nineveh, a great city full of people, was spiraling out of control due to wickedness. God chose Jonah, the prophet, to warn them to repent or be overthrown. However, ole arrogant Jonah did not want the task. Instead, he decided to ignore God. Doing this jeopardized innocent lives, and God had to show him who was actually in charge. Jonah was temporarily humbled by three days of frightening isolation, one would think. He goes to Nineveh and warns the people as God commanded, but once again he's overcome with arrogance and complains because Almighty God decided not to destroy the people. He thought, 'You knew this all the time, and I went through this for what?' Kids, I know you've heard this story over and over, but I need to paint a picture for you. God exercised a tremendous amount of patience with Jonah, but more importantly, God chose Jonah."

He then turned to his family and asked, "Why do you think I am telling you this story? You see, if God presents you with a task, it may be out of your comfort zone, or you might become arrogant and say, 'God, I'll pass this one up!' We've all been guilty. Unfortunately, you run the risk of disobedience. It's crucial to trust God and leave the details to Him whether you comprehend the end result or not. We are all instruments of God, and while helping others, we accomplish His will. We, the Haugens, were chosen for this task. Let's honor God. Andrew and Peter, I'm asking the both of you to continue to pray because believe it or not, I need the two of you and Sarah. We've always worked through our challenges, and this is no exception. I'm trusting God to take me in a new direction. I'm going to help those folks and spread the Word of God."

Helen teared up and went to her husband.

"Andrew and Pete, Dad is pragmatic, and if he says it's God's will, then it's His will. Who are we to go against that? He knows how uncomfortable I am around gays, probably more so than you two. God knows my heart. I don't hate them. I just don't want to be around them. So, Dad, I know you will figure this out, and I believe God will protect us. That's all I'm going to say for now."

"Okay, Dad, what's the plan in a nutshell? Bottom line," asked Peter.

"Peter, you just said being too close to the fire. I say with God's grace, you walk through the fire. Nate is the overseeing attorney who would assist me with the Luccia House."

"So you've now gone from thinking about it to actually taking it on?" Andrew added.

"Here's the plan in a nutshell. The location of this facility is in Tiburon, right outside of San Francisco. Helen doesn't know about this, but I plan to include a chapel at the location with Sunday service and daily Bible classes. I spoke with your mom earlier, and it's worth mentioning again that as Christians, everyone is worthy to be saved, and that is the Great Commission Christ left the disciples. I plan to add a subtitle referencing God under the Luccia House."

"Dan was an atheist, and my father the pastor is a major player in the Luccia House, a place for the aging gay, and this is your bottom line plan, Dad? Well, with that much money, please be sure to hire a Christian PR firm. God in heaven knows you will need one," said Andrew sarcastically.

"Presentation is everything. If not, we will be called hypocrites, or even worse, sellouts. Yeah, Haugen sellouts!" added Peter sorrowfully.

Pastor Haugen mused.

"I don't know for sure. This is only my theory, and keep in mind, I didn't know him. Dan knew dozens of people to appoint over the Luccia House. Politicians, artist, and people in entertainment—something was lacking that impeded him in choosing someone. Think about it. His mother was a very spiritual Christian. Dan was a Christian growing up and became an atheist after he felt God turned his back on him. It happens, and most come back to their senses. How was Dan going to appoint a spiritual person over the Luccia House without crossing his atheist boundaries? He was in a quandary."

In absolute frustration, Pastor Haugen let out a large sigh. "Call it a quandary. It was his, not yours. Not ours!" added Andrew angrily.

"Kids, it wasn't an accident their car stalled. It was a miracle all around. Yes, I said it, honey. Who better than the Haugens to spend time with Cane just hours before he passed away and provide his family with loving memories. It probably wouldn't have happened with anyone else. Cane's last hours on earth, he was laughing and feeling freedom. Of course, there was a hiccup—that's what Satan does.

Who better than the Haugens to spend time with Dan just hours before he passed away? He embraced a grounded Christian family who opened their home to strangers and discovered we are loving, caring people serving the Lord. We shared our stories of a group of us going to Haiti to help rebuild, our annual Winter Clothes for Kids campaign and how all of us are regular volunteers at the homeless kitchen. We were that spiritual piece to an ever-building puzzle God designed. Look at this as being a miracle from God. He wants the Haugens, not just your father, but this entire family."

Helen was extremely emotional and began to tear up, and Anders walked over and hugged her. She knew her husband's confidence, facing any opposition outside the family, would be strengthened by fierce internal support, so she poured out her soul to the children.

"Let us not forget that we can't control people, only our actions toward them. Every time I read the newspapers, another layer of homosexuality is unfurling, and I get disgusted. It's the world we live in. Change always begins with a thought and then an action. Last I checked, if God be for you, who can be against you?"

"Amen, honey."

"Let me finish, Anders. Kids, this is only one in many of life's challenges. You are young, and if it's God's will you live as old as us, you will have story after story of how God Almighty brought you through, and add this to your list. Hold your heads up high, believe in your father, and trust your Heavenly Father."

"Thank you, Helen."

"No. Thank God. He alone."

"Don't forget, kids, I plan to bring God front and center as, perhaps, Luccia Piattoni would have done. Remember, God did not send his Son into the world to condemn the world, but to save the world through him. Let's save some folks and offer a beautiful place to live in. Honestly, I plan to see it through and step aside, not be actively involved in the daily operations but only establishing a foundation. Take your focus off Dan and onto his mother and what she represented. This brings a different dynamic to the situation. He was only an instrument, as we all are."

"You never know what God has planned. If your reactions are any inclination as to what's in store, we're in for a rough ride. This is only one discussion out of many more to come. Andrew and Peter, help your father."

She kissed him on the cheeks and extended her hand out to the kids. Sarah walked up to her parents and looked at her brothers, and one by one, they huddled together.

"Thank you, Lord. Thank you," said Pastor Haugen.

"As a family, let's see where God is leading us. When we get back home, I will contact Nate and gather some information on Luccia Piattoni. Once we discover who she was, then we can begin building this legacy. The Luccia House is the legal and only name permitted, which I plan to honor. However, I'm thinking about adding a subtitle in remembrance of some sort or indicating its foundation is Christian, maybe something on the lines of 'a place where God is love.'"

"Oh, wow! You can do better than that. Really, Dad?" Peter sarcastically said.

"What about 'He will be with you always'?" Sarah added.

"Sis, this isn't an obituary reading. It's a legacy. Jeez!" Peter added.

"Okay, I'll chime in on this one. What about 'The Luccia House, a place where God's love abides.'"

"Mom, it sounds just like Dad's."

"All right, Peter, what would you add?" asked Helen.

"Give me a minute. These things take time."

"Duh. Ask him in six months. I've got one," chimed in Andrew.

In astonishment to Andrew's participation, Pastor Haugen and Helen looked at one another.

"Okay, son, go for it!" said Pastor Haugen.

"The Luccia House—her faith and love for God lives on through her spirit."

Helen was flabbergasted and placed her hands across her chest and said, "Oh my goodness, you never cease to amaze me. It's perfect. Honey, what do you think?"

"I agree. It's perfect. Now let's see if I can legally add it."

"It's good, Andrew," said Sarah.

"I must admit, bro, you nailed it. Dad, use it as a bargaining chip when you speak to Mr. Piattoni's attorney. I don't think you'll have a problem."

"We'll see. Remember, as I said earlier, this is only one of many challenges to come. Not so fast, everyone. I didn't forget about blessings."

"I will go first again," said Helen. "We are blessed to be able to disagree, express our opinions, get angry, yet at the end of the day realize we are a family who pulls together and is Christ-centered."

"My turn," added Peter. "I'm blessed to know that miracles don't necessarily happen with the obvious."

"Andrew? Sarah?"

"I'll go, Dad," replied Andrew. "The blessing—not to allow fear to control your thinking about consequences you don't have control over."

Pastor Haugen gestured to Sarah.

"I hope to remember when I'm an adult that when bad things happen, especially to Christians, it may be much later on until you see God's blessing from the incident."

"Wow! Helen, I think our kids are really growing up. What do you think?"

Helen shook her head.

"Your mother asked me to wait a couple of days and pray more about sharing the Luccia House with you, and I'm happy I listened to her. Death and odd circumstances with their blessings will happen throughout your lives. I pray you hold these life lessons close to your heart to draw down some wisdom. It builds character. I'd like to close in a prayer."

The Haugens formed a hand-holding circle.

"Heavenly Father, thank you for all your many blessings, knowing and unknowing. Thank you for giving me the wisdom and courage to share the latest project, the Luccia House, with my family. I'm thankful for my wife and kids that we are able to disagree, share, and remain steadfast as a family. Thank you for the trials that test and build our character as it provides an opportunity for us to further understand one another. Thank you for your gentleness in exposing this family to an unbeliever who, only through you, proved to be a blessing. I ask that you continue to guide and protect this family in your truths. We know that challenges are on our path, but more importantly, you've gone on before us. With faith in you, we know you will not give us anything that we aren't able to handle, as written in your Holy Word of First Corinthians. Father God, shower this family with joy and peace as our tradition is wrapping up. May we enjoy and appreciate the surrounding beauty of South Lake Tahoe. It is in your Son Jesus Christ's name we pray, let us all say, Amen."

And so, it was prior to returning to Elk Grove for the New Year over the next couple of days that the Haugens finally began to enjoy their traditional vacation with relaxation, snowboarding, and skiing.

Daniel Piattoni and Jeffrey Cane Peters, two strangers, entered their lives and changed them profoundly forever. And through death, it was revealed the two friends were actually strangers among themselves.

THE ELDER'S ENIGMA

The Haugens arrived home safely from their traditional retreat, celebrated the New Year, and resumed their post-holiday schedules. Pastor Haugen had the support of his entire family, howbeit their honest reservations. He and Helen spent a considerable time discussing the best way to convey his plans first to the four elders of the church and finally to the congregation.

The meeting was scheduled with the elders at five on Wednesday (Bible class began at seven). Their final thought was for him to tell the entire story exactly how it happened, his reluctance, the Jonah syndrome, and intense prayers. He had a solid amicable relationship with each of the elders. His three children's reactions to the Luccia House, in his mind, was highly indicative of what was to be expected by the congregation as a whole.

To avoid any sidebar conversations among themselves, he refrained from disclosing the subject matter, even when he was tempted immediately returning from South Lake Tahoe.

Silver Rock Christian Center
Wednesday at 4:50 p.m.

As he entered the driveway, one of the elders noticed him and patiently waited.

"Hello, Anders! How are you?" asked Marcus Childs.

"Fine, doing just fine," replied Pastor Haugen.

"What about yourself? How's your back?"

"Simply by His grace, and the old back is the old back. What can I say? It's been supporting me for seventy-seven years."

They both laughed and walked into his office. In Pastor Haugen's office, there was a small conference table that seated six comfortably—all were present.

"Hello, brethren. Thank you for rearranging your schedules to meet with me today. Let's begin with a word of prayer so I can move this along."

After the prayer, he briefly looked at everyone at the table. "During our vacation, something happened to our entire family. Nothing bad per se, but it profoundly impacted the Haugens, and it will impact this congregation as well. I ask that you please listen before commenting. It will take you aback. I've decided to take on a controversial project, and I'm praying for your support. God knows I will need it."

The introductory comment established a serious tone, and the group was more inquisitive about the secret as ever. Pastor Haugen nervously began to tell how Daniel Piattoni, Jeffrey Cane Peters, Nathaniel Horowitz, Pastor Peters, the Luccia House, and the robust five percent of the forty-four million dollars entered and exited their lives.

Their expressions loomed back and forth from stoic to amazement until toward the end, utter bewilderment.

"Brethren, there you have it, and I don't believe I've left any rock unturned. I'm now ready for questions, comments." He was afforded with sighs, rubbing of heads, and leaning back in their seats.

"Son, you plan to add a chapel to this project?" asked Elder Childs.

"Yes, sir. Mr. Horowitz agreed that shouldn't be an issue."

"I will say, Anders, God often doesn't look at the circumstance, but the outcome of His will."

Questions and comments continued until it was 6:40. There was no offensive idiosyncratic outburst. The ultimate gift of wisdom and understanding from God's called humbled his overly apprehensive spirit.

"I've been in the church all my life, and many times I've witnessed how God's plan is carried out through our muck and mire of life. Anders, we've come to know you fairly well across the years, and if you believe this is your calling, you have my blessing," added Elder Leslie Oliver, whom Pastor Haugen believed would be his guaranteed critic. He was emotionally overcome by the statement.

Elder Childs nodded in agreement. Elder John Hines stood up and walked over and stroked his back.

"How is your family doing in all of this?" he asked.

"It was a rough start, as I mentioned. They're depending on me to get this right. I don't want to disappoint them—or anyone, for that matter."

Elder Bartholomew Pena reached over and shook his hand.

"Son, God will protect you and this congregation. It will be a good work, and we know that all things work together for the good of those who are called according to his purpose. Don't worry! We are here to support you! Let us know when you want to call a church meeting, preferably a Saturday. Let us be responsible for easing their minds."

"Thank you all so much. I needed your support, and now I feel confident about my decision. Honestly, I just didn't know what to expect."

"May I suggest you communicate with us regularly," stated Elder Childs.

"Absolutely. With the added funding coming our way, we are going to be busy building His kingdom."

"Amen." added Elder Hines.

Elder Oliver led a closing prayer. Pastor Haugen left the meeting empowered and prepared to face the new assignment in his life.

Three weeks later, a church meeting was held. Pastor Haugen asked his family to refrain from sharing any details with others. Elder Leslie Oliver opened the meeting by stating they supported the pastor and his family with the decision to become involved in the extraordinary project. Pastor Haugen stood at the podium with Helen and the kids at his side.

As he began to share detail after detail, you could hear a pin drop. At the conclusion, when everyone was pleased and accepting of the new venture, he ends by adding Dan's sexual orientation—the game changer. A microphone was passed around for nearly two hours with all the familiar questions previously asked by his family and the elders, which served him well as a practice run for the congregation. It was eerily civil. There was murmuring, but no objective outburst, smug expressions, or walkouts. Pastor Haugen thought surely someone was going to behave out of character and yet no one.

Afterward, all the elders stood with a compassionate plea for the sake of unity to not engage in divisive conversations or acts but instead to seek their council.

THE DEMISE OF INTENT

In San Francisco, the Horowitz Law Firm was located atop a renovated building that looked out to the Bay Bridge and Treasure Island. This location afforded a priceless view of boats sailing and the occasional yachts. The irresistible synergy drew people from all around the world. Nate's chic office was decorated with contemporary art complemented with panache colors.

Pastor Haugen and Nate met informally two weeks after leaving South Lake Tahoe to share some preliminary ideas such as the subtitle and the addition of a chapel to the project. Nate had no problem with the subtitle addition to the Luccia House. As a matter of fact, he agreed it represented the spirit of the late Luccia Piattoni.

Six weeks after Daniel Piattoni's death…
February 10, 2015
4:00 p.m.

Nate contacted all the major beneficiaries (excluding two foundations) of the reading of Dan's will—Pastor Anders Haugen, Ingrid Livingston, Thomas Lee Seymore, and Jonathan Murphy. In times past, his experience made him the wiser to know that marriages and funerals created either friends or foes. Wills are particularly difficult when large sums of money and people with preconceived notions of benevolence are involved. This group of friends would not be any different, especially with Pastor Haugen officially accepting to lead the Luccia House.

The meeting would take place in half an hour in conference room one. Helen decided to accompany her husband to the meeting. They arrived first. They were led to the conference room by the receptionist, and soft jazz was playing over the intercom.

"You know, California has some spectacular views," said Pastor Haugen.

"This is why people love it here," added Helen. "How long do you suppose the meeting will last?"

"Not sure at all. I'm guessing an hour."

"Hello, Pastor Haugen!" said Nate.

"Good afternoon, Nate!"

"Good afternoon!" Helen responded.

"You must be Mrs. Haugen!"

"Yes, nice to meet you. After all these weeks, I finally have the opportunity to meet the infamous Nathaniel Horowitz."

"My pleasure."

"Good afternoon, everyone," said Thomas.

Thomas and Jonathan met one another on the elevator, and Jonathan mentioned he saw Ingrid drive into the garage as he was entering. Nate offered water, coffee, and wine as everyone took a seat and waited for Ingrid. Ingrid arrived, and the meeting began.

His secretary entered the room, set a stack of burgundy portfolio binders at his side, and left, closing the door.

"I'd like to thank each of you for agreeing to meet at this time for the reading of Daniel Piattoni's will. As the executor of the estate, the two foundations, Meiner and Woodhouse, have been notified, and they will not be present. However, after this meeting, their copies will be hand-delivered." Then he began reading the will. "To Ingrid Livingston, you were the sister I never had. I leave you the Healing Home. Please make new fond memories, and may joy and peace be your forever companions."

Ingrid cried and smiled.

"To my neighbor and dear friend, Jonathan Murphy, I leave you my entire music collection and the Fazioli piano. Also, when I recently sold the property in Nice, I had all of my parents' music sent home—it's yours as well. Most are in Italian. Enjoy!"

Jonathan was completely overjoyed, and he smiled.

"To my kindred spirit, Thomas Lee Seymore, the teacher's teacher and the love of children and music, I leave you one hundred thousand dollars to open a small studio to continue your passion to teach music to the brightest talent we found in the darkest places. The two foundations will support you with modest quarterly stipends. Inspire, dear friend!"

Thomas stood up, took a bow, and said rather loudly, "Yes! Thank you, Daniel Piattoni."

"Dan modified his will a few months ago. If the three of you remember, when Dan was hospitalized, I asked you to leave Dan and me alone. He was still modifying on his deathbed. To Pastor Anders Haugen, a courageous man of God, an honorable man, I want you to be the chief executive officer of the forty-four-million-dollar Luccia House project. Your missionary projects and love for people will make it a success despite the obstacles. Prove them wrong!"

Pastor Haugen broke a modest smile as he and Helen held hands. Thomas, Jonathan, and Ingrid were all taken aback.

"What? He's leaving him in charge of the Luccia House! This is absurd! This isn't true. It can't be. Someone tell me I'm dreaming. Nate, what are you attempting to pull off here?" shouted Ingrid.

"Really? Are you kidding? He didn't know this man," said Thomas.

Jonathan, however, was quiet.

"No, no. I wandered why you were here at this reading. There needs to be some explaining here. Month after month, every detail we could possibly fathom we discussed. I agree with Thomas. You

Ms. Pamela

didn't even know Dan. What's going on here, Nate? Why are you betraying Dan?" added Ingrid as she cried.

"Please compose yourself and lower your voice, Ingrid. Please. Let me finish," Nate said in a raised voice.

"Thomas and Ingrid, this was all conveyed prior to Dan being hospitalized. As the executor of his estate and dear friend, I have no need to lie and, God forbid, do something unethical. How dare you even insinuate."

"What do you expect me to do? You mean to tell me Dan meets this gentleman and in the span of a couple of hours leaves a forty-four-million-dollar Luccia House project to him? You've got to be kidding me. Really? Really, Nate? You are lying, and he's in on it! A pastor!"

"I beg your pardon!" said Helen.

Nate stood up and, in an agitated voice, said, "That's enough, Ingrid. I will overlook the fact that you've blatantly accused me of being unethical. Sit down and listen or leave. Your decision."

"What do you take me for? Do you really think I will leave here without getting to the truth?"

"Then please sit down and listen."

She angrily peered at Pastor Haugen and Nate.

"Everyone, turn to page four, line eleven. Read for yourselves."

Pages turned, and the revelation of the mysterious request shocked Ingrid, Thomas, and Jonathan.

"This is why Pastor Haugen was requested by Dan. Pastor Haugen initially wanted nothing to do with this project. We had a few choice words. Remember, Pastor Haugen?"

He smiled.

"The Luccia House is larger than anyone in this room. Look around. Each of us brings a unique inspiring quality to this project. We are the inner circle. We need one another for the Luccia House to be successful and, more importantly, to be the way Dan

– 156 –

envisioned this meaningful endeavor. Pastor Haugen, Helen, and I have discussed a couple of changes or additions, I should say, to complement the Luccia House. Pastor Haugen, please." Nate gestured for him to speak.

"I've heard some incredible stories about Luccia Piattoni. She was spiritual, loving, and compassionate. She looked for the beauty in people. For Dan to have worked so diligently to leave a legacy not for his name but his mother goes beyond mere words. To enhance and truly epitomize her spirit, we plan to add a chapel and a subtitle to the Luccia House. On the building, letterhead, etcetera, it will read, 'The Luccia House—her faith and love for God lives on through her spirit.'"

Ingrid sarcastically clapped slowly.

"Oh my. By the way, Pastor Haugen and my dear friend Nate, you both left out one insignificant minor detail. How do you plan to spearhead a gay project when you don't believe in a gay lifestyle?" she added.

"I'm truly flabbergasted and blown away with everything that has transpired here, but Ingrid, I must, say raises a valid point," said Thomas.

"I'm listening as well," added Jonathan.

"It's no secret I don't believe in homosexuality, and I am a follower of Christ. I'm not wavering from this position. And in the same voice, I will not turn my back on people who need help. I don't plan to manage the day-to-day operations of the Luccia House ever. However, I do plan to establish some Christian ground work for those who are seeking God. It is indicative of Luccia Piattoni."

"You two can sit here all nonchalant if you chose, but Dan was an atheist, and all of us in this room respected him, even though we didn't agree. A chapel!"

"To be honest here, okay, he was not the norm, but it was a chapel I could envision him adding. It makes perfect sense to me. It's not my call. I guess I can live with the subtitle," added Thomas.

"Let's make sure we're all on the same page here. The subtitle and the chapel for the Luccia House, to be honest, is privileged information as far as I'm concerned. I shared it in this meeting as a courtesy and nothing more. I don't require or need your feedback or any opinion you've formulated. I shared merely as a courtesy to Dan's close friends so that down the road when you heard about these specific ideas, you would not feel unease about not knowing. Further, Ingrid, let's keep in mind that while, yes, Dan was an atheist, both his parents were Christians. You and I both know Dan said his mother prayed all the time, so the idea of modifying the plans to include a chapel is not extraordinary. On his deathbed, I gave a solemn oath to my dear friend that his plans will be honored, and this, Ms. Ingrid, I plan to do, not you. Capiche!"

She mused.

Jonathan looked at Ingrid and shook his head.

"Ingrid, I still can't get over the fact he's gone, that's one issue. Dan didn't maintain his millions by making poor decisions. It seemed to me everything he touched turned to gold. Some things he shared about how he pulled them off were absolutely baffling, and now it's neither here nor there. The second issue is that his reasons for appointing Pastor Haugen are buried right along with him. So there you have it. Let's accept the obvious and move on. Too much negative energy will hinder your healing," said Jonathan.

"Ingrid, please don't do this. We've all known Nate for as long as we knew Dan. This is what Dan wanted, for God's sake. It's in writing. Odd, yes, but still true. Dan was always encouraging us to seek peace with our sources, which included primarily Christianity. We all knew about the Luccia House, and who's to say what it would have evolved into had he lived. A place for the aged and dying…Who's to say he wasn't actively seeking a spiritual person to head this? And why do you seem to be so damn bitter when you, my dear, have the Healing Home? That was his heart. Please! Or do you feel you should have been the one overseeing the Luccia

House? If that were the case, trust me, he would have appointed you some time ago, and the fact remains that he didn't! Darling, it's time to get over yourself. Mrs. Haugen, Pastor Haugen, and everyone, excuse us for the minor slipup," said Thomas.

"Get over myself. I'm here to defend Dan. Seems no one else will."

Before another syllable was uttered, Nate interrupted. "I've provided everyone with their necessary copies of the will. I will end by saying we've all lost a great friend, and the void we now have will never be replaced. He cared deeply for people, not in the moment, but in the long term. Let's leave here honoring his legacy with the generous means he bequeathed to empower all of us to do so."

He continued, "Reservations are at five-thirty in Sausalito at Dan's favorite restaurant, and the limousine awaits. If there aren't any further concerns or issues, this meeting is over, and we can be on our way to continue celebrating his life."

Small talk ensued, and both Jonathan and Thomas offered their services at any stage of the project to Pastor Haugen and Helen. Nate was pleased and not at all surprised by their gestures.

The dinner in Sausalito was a successful mini meet-and-greet. All were engaged, with the exception of Ingrid, who remained socially polite yet reserved. True to its very being, the Luccia House proved to be the pink elephant in the room that was avoided with finesse.

INGRID'S LETTER OF DISCONTENTMENT

One week after the reading of the will, a letter addressed to Pastor Haugen arrived in the mail. Helen immediately determined it was from Ingrid and notifies her husband at the church. His suspicions were leading him to believe it was a legal document to stop or hinder his legal right over the Luccia House. Helen asked if he would prefer that she open and read it, but he declined. Instead, they would read it together after dinner and not before. That evening, the couple went into their office.

"Helen, it's a letter, not a legal document."

"That's a relief. Lord knows what she has to say. I'm sure it isn't filled with pleasantries."

"Here, you read it."

February 26, 2015

Dear Pastor Anders Haugen,

It is with the sincerest of intentions to write you and express my utter dismay of your handling of my beloved friend's, the late Daniel Piattoni, Luccia House project in memory of his mother, the late Mrs. Luccia Piattoni. For the record, I respect the outcome of Dan selecting you as the person to proceed with bringing his dream to fruition.

I knew Dan for many, many years prior to his passing, and I know, as a matter of fact, that I consider myself to be one of the few people who knew him personally. We shared our triumphs, trials, and dreams. I was the very first person to know about the Luccia House. He shared with me story after story about his mother and how she impacted his life. Her love, graciousness, and kindness toward others personified her legacy. She spoiled and loved him more than life itself. The time as a young adult when he was separated from his mother, he told me it was as if he was living in a black hole, not able to touch or see. How he was robbed from seeing her during the last few days of her life disturbed him until his death. Again, he shared all of this with me as his best friend.

All people have idiosyncrasies about themselves, and Dan was no exception. First a Christian, then an atheist. Odd, but it was his business. He detested institutional religion because leaders demanded their flocks to adhere to their own communal and ritualistic thinking, and true religion played a miniscule role. He experienced how man could love God totally on one hand and hate his brother on the other, knowing full well this is not God's commandment. Mr. Alonso Piattoni, Dan's father, was this example. As long as you do as I say, I will love you. If you don't, I will disown you. This last punitive action convinced Dan that God was orchestrating this same trait, and there he turned and walked away from his life-long belief. I didn't agree, but I understood his position.

I believe God is in my heart, and I don't need some demanding leader to bury me with guilt in order to fill Sunday's pews without knowing my personal walk, sign forms stating how much I will give for the year, or any other embattling legalistic order of service.

Now my point, a spiritual leader as yourself is given a once-in-a-lifetime opportunity to offer love and gracious comfort to people on a grand scale, and instead of keeping it simple, you become counterintuitive by making it your own recognizable mantra. God! God! God! If the Luccia House is exactly what it should be, there will be no need for subtitled reminders. It should speak for itself through his mother's true spirit, compassion, and grace. You don't demand it; it will command itself.

It is also my understanding you are placing a chapel in the facility. Is it your plan to convert all the residents? Dan never mentioned this in any of our conversations. People on their dying beds or alone don't require any coercion to religion. Are you going to add a stipulation that as a resident you must attend the chapel? I pray not. What would Dan say to all of your modifications if he could speak from the grave?

It is my opinion to appease your own circle of friends/critics or whoever you needed to put your God spin on it to show you were in control. For this, I'm completely appalled. Again, for the record, this does not speak to the spirits of Daniel and Luccia Piattoni, but Pastor Anders Haugen.

The truth spoken from my heart,

Ms. Ingrid Livingston.

"Anders, you need to talk to her."

"Ingrid is still very much in shock about losing Dan, who was like a brother to her. Anger is part of the grieving process, and I don't want to agitate an already volatile situation. She's grasping at straws."

"That woman has accused you of being some narcissistic money-seeking person. She's clueless, and maybe not now but sometime soon a conversation must take place. I can meet with her."

"No."

"We'll let the work speak for itself. Wasn't it you who told me it's none of my business what people think about me?"

"Touché. Are you saying none of this bothers you?"

"What I'm saying is right now I don't have time to sweat the small stuff. I've got this additional assignment, and if I get sidetracked every time someone has an emotional tantrum, I'll eventually lose my focus. Nate mentioned she and Dan went to the Healing Home frequently during the summer. Hopefully, that's where her true healing can begin."

THE LUCCIA HOUSE

Nate arranged for the five of the informal "inner circle," including himself, to tour the property of the proposed site. This was an emotional gathering, knowing Dan did not live to see his dream become a reality. Only he could have selected such a stunning and secluded location. The old property was tucked away in an area off the beaten path with distant views of the San Francisco Bay. The planned expansion of the property was designed to respect the environment, thus, not disturbing too much of the mature landscape.

The groundbreaking for the Luccia House took place four weeks after the reading of the will. Pastor Haugen and Helen did not attend the ceremony—he was officially a silent partner, if you will. It was upsetting and at times totally unacceptable to the others that Pastor Haugen remained so low-key given the enormity of his role. However, Nate understood his position completely. After all, the method in which Dan chose him was as unorthodox as the manner in which Pastor Haugen was leading the charge of the Luccia House.

At the start, they complained incessantly to Nate about anything and everything—him not being present, especially with the five-percent payment he was receiving, but eventually it tapered off. Nate chalked it up to being a tad envious. It was baffling at times even to him how Dan knew Pastor Haugen was meticulously detail-oriented, pragmatic, and technically astute. He had a no-

nonsense business approach that quietened the complaining and ultimately acquired their respect. Pastor Haugen once a week conducted site visits, and Helen and the kids joined him when schedules permitted.

Eleven months later…
The Luccia House

The grand opening was attended by politicians, quite a few from the art community, and many of Dan's old friends. As Pastor Haugen alluded to from the onset, he did not attend, but he and Helen were front and center with the planning.

The Luccia House was a twenty-one-unit facility with a resort style of living. There was a state-of-the art small medical office for the part-time volunteer physicians. Each one-bedroom unit has solid wood flooring, bookshelves, a complete kitchen, full-size digital washer and dryer, and French doors leading into the bedroom.

It was equipped with a state-of-the-art commercial kitchen with an Italian flair, dining area, and a common area with an open pit fireplace located outside. The intimate chapel was a masterpiece. The ornate crown molding and intricate detailing were designed by the best. An oversized stain glass window with a brown cross draped in purple was the focal point. There were four rows of pews on each side for a small service. So as not to be confined to the grounds, one mile down the road there was a walking trail and bike route.

A seven-member board was appointed by Nate and Pastor Haugen—quite an arduous task. Thomas, Jonathan, and, of course, Ingrid would serve. In all fairness, it was agreed upon to advertise locally, but word quickly spread, and they received applications from around the country. A lottery system was used to determine the first round of residents, and a waiting list was, thus, established. Thomas had agreed to have regular musical performances from his students. The Luccia House Volunteer Program established and managed by Ingrid and Jonathan received requests to volunteer from physicians, landscaping to art classes, and it was amazing.

Pastor Haugen remained steadfast in his beliefs and followed God through prayer as he was led on this unusual assignment. It was not without its share of challenges, but thanks be to the glory of God, it was completed. This experience increased his entire family's faith in God by Pastor Haugen leading the example of learning not to compromise His Word—stand boldly, wait and watch God's masterful plan unfold, even if you feel you are alone.

He was true to his word, no mega church here. He did not lose one church member. As a matter of fact, his membership increased. He paid off the church mortgage with still a large sum placed in the kid's college fund and built a church and a Christian school in Haiti and Kenya for the missionary work. He had prayed year after year for God to help him succeed with his missionaries, and it far exceeded his expectations. "Now to him who is able to do far more abundantly beyond all that we ask or think, according to the power that works within us" (Eph. 3:20).

After the Luccia House was completed, plans were in the works to take the family on a once-in-a-lifetime vacation out of the country. How could anyone comprehend that a simple kind act to assist absolute strangers would conceive such a project and continue to bring strangers together for the common good to help others in need? Only the one true living God and his mystery of miracles.

IN THINKING
(SIGNATURE CHAPTER)

The Word of God has not changed; however, the presentation of the Word has and is changing concurrently with time. "As also in all his epistles, speaking in them of these things, in which are some things hard to understand, which untaught and unstable people twist to their own destruction, as they do also the rest of the Scriptures" (2 Pet. 3:16).

First and foremost, I believe God created man and woman with this specific sexual institution—not man for man or woman for woman. I've heard and continue to hear this old adage, "What would Jesus do if He were here?" Personally, I believe this is oftentimes overly used and rated. Must I remind all fellow saints that the Holy Spirit indwells within us and will be with us always? Is not this the mind and spirit of God? We have become much more fearful of man than God by continually adhering to our culture's political corrects and abhorring our Heavenly Father's spiritual directs.

As a citizen of the United States of America, the most democratic society on the planet, rights and freedoms are blood-sewn in our flag and constitution. I adamantly don't agree with our country's Neo-God sexual orientation; however, I will continue to pray, exercise Godly love, respect, and remain committed to not mistreating individuals who have made this informed decision.

In our country, we exercise freedom and are encouraged to create like-minded environments such as schools, churches, programs, organizations, etc. I vote based on my values, and when laws are mandated, I obey. I experienced racism and sexism by Christians who believe in the same God I worship. These individuals were resolute in behaving in deliberate opposition to not only the constitution but also the Word of God.

Furthermore, as a citizen of heaven, no matter how difficult it is, or even if I feel justified to not love, I am commanded to love. "Teacher, which is the greatest commandment in the Law?" Jesus replied, "Love the Lord your God with all your heart and with all your soul and with all your mind. This is the first and greatest commandment. And the second is like it. Love your neighbor as yourself. All the Law and the Prophets hang on these two commandments" (Matt. 22:36–40).

Many spiritual leaders, ministers, pastors, and bishops have not devised a biblical plan of action for interaction with homosexuals in their congregations other than preaching it's wrong—how wounding to His name is this?—oftentimes believing they will dodge this bullet. Our culture is too intelligent and sophisticated for this most elementary form of teaching to just say, "No!"

The Word has substantive history, examples, cause, long-term consequences, and, more importantly, deliverance to preach an advanced compelling message. The somber truth is that many have children or close relatives who step forward as homosexuals, and it is no longer a pulpit issue but a personal conflict. Without saying, we love our children dearly and do our absolute best in raising and holding them in high regard—it's natural. However, when their personal choices blindside us, you hear statements like "I'm not going to judge!" or "It's their life!" as surface statements to block entry into a more complex relationship, opting, if at all possible, to remain private.

Established and storefront pulpits throughout America are striving for money, nepotism, power, and pew-filling, thus, conflicting with the message of our Lord but aligning with a capitalistic mindset. They believe the Neo-God of today is not the same God since creation and dismiss scriptures, replacing commandment with conciliatory and, more importantly, replacing the Holy Spirit with feel-good-only dogma and prosperity preaching. As teachers of the Word, we are set apart. "My brethren, let not many of you become teachers, knowing that we should receive a stricter judgment" (James 3:1).

The imminent threat of altering scripture based on social trends and the fearful messenger being overly cognizant not to offend is paradoxical. One scripture in particular comes to mind that commands and warns. "I testify to everyone who hears the words of the prophecy of this book: if anyone adds to them, God will add to him the plaques which are written in this book; and if anyone takes away from this words of the book of this prophecy, God will take away his part from the tree of life and from the holy city, which are written in the book" (Rev. 22:18–19).

Most homosexual Christians believe God understands and accepts their orientation unconditionally. Many adamantly profess God would not have created them as a homosexual if it was unacceptable to Him, believing He's not that unloving or unreasonable. Gay-only churches are mounting because of acceptance issues in traditional congregations and the general need to feel comfortable worshipping God. A gay Christian can valiantly take a stand, jeopardizing family and friend ties, reputation, position, and anything else of significant value in support of their sexual preference.

How many instances have I seen time and time again church leaders who appeared on large public forums, smiling guardedly to their host with circumvented answers of their belief in homosexuality? It is no longer a mystery to me how the Apostles denied our Lord and Savior the night he was taken captive. They witnessed people raised from the dead, the blind whose sight restored, and demonic spirits called out of people. Was it the spirit of rejection? Or was it the spirit of fear? It was a combination of both. This spirit of rejection is one of the most powerful demonic spirits consciously feared by man, and it goes back to the core of our human nature being accepted. The spirits of rejection and fear combined will cause an intelligent God-fearing person to consider their potential tangible losses and how they are viewed by people, consequently giving no credence to "What profit a man to gain the whole world and lose his soul?" (Matt. 16:26). We know this scripture means that if a man acquires great wealth and nobility, it is incomparable to the value of one's soul if lost.

Examine yourselves daily as commanded and remember all of us will be held accountable for our deeds in this life. "Don't you realize that those who do wrong will not inherit the Kingdom of God? Don't fool yourselves. Those who indulge in sexual sin, who worship idols, prostitutes, or practice homosexuality" (1 Cor. 6:9). Based on this scripture, an excellent reference point is that homosexuality is *a* sin, and not *the* sin.

No, I am not downplaying homosexuality, but God's focus is always on the inward man, the spirit. I will go so far as to say the seven deadly sins did not include homosexuality, "There are six things the Lord hates, seven that are detestable to Him: haughty eyes, a lying tongue, hands that shed innocent blood, a heart that devises wicked schemes, feet that are quick to rush into evil, a false witness who pours out lies, and a man who stirs up dissension among brothers" (Prov. 6:16–19).

Remembering as a young teenager, one Saturday night, a male relative frantically knocked on our back door, almost storming it down. I rushed to see who it was, and as I peered through the curtain, he incessantly began yelling, pushing the door, and turning the knob. As I opened the door, he violently pushed me aside, stumbled to the other side, and turned off the kitchen light while swearing hysterically. A carful of guys drove, dawdling down the street, and we knew without asking they were looking for him. As my siblings fell into rank, not one of us asked what had happened. With unwavering certainty, had that group sited him in our home, all of us would have fought them tooth and nail to defend his safety. I was furious thinking, how dare you, heathens.

We knew he was flamboyantly gay, and yet our family allowed this pink elephant in the room to dwell always. He was our blood relative whom we loved dearly, and we looked past any obscurities in his character. Perhaps, youth and the times cloaked our naïve impressionable minds from this dichotomy of life.

Does God Love Everyone?

Many ministers and pastors preach, "I don't' care if you are straight, gay, black, white, or whatever. God loves you, and so do we." Again, God does love everyone. These statements make people feel inclusive, and they tell a portion of the truth, but not the whole. "Preach the word; be prepared in season and out of season; correct, rebuke and encourage—with great patience and careful instruction" (2 Tim. 4:2). Preaching an unfavorable sermon is daunting, especially when you are calculative of offending, and it is "out of season."

"God loves everyone" is a globally referenced statement and transcends all languages and cultures. However, the truth be told, when we move further into wisdom and understanding, the fullness reveals a loving God, and with this love comes commandments.

Daniel Piattoni was genuinely a good person by all accounts. His established philanthropic reputation was ongoing. Aside from the traditional holiday giving, he was astutely grounded in the arts and regionally known as an advocate for the underserved and disadvantaged people. Howbeit, he remained outside the will of God, perhaps, until his last breath was taken. When Dan revealed his sexual orientation to his father, he was rejected, and this rejection resulted in misdirected anger that led to a period of an irresponsible and reckless lifestyle. Dan admitted this was how he contracted AIDS.

Cane, in his drunken state, committed an immoral sexual act. He basically made a life-altering mistake. He yearned for what was innately within him, and it crystallized when his path crossed with the Haugen family. Unfortunately, man condemned him over and over to the point of hopelessness, and ultimately it led to his and someone else's death. But God had immediately forgiven him when he asked.

Dan brought up a valid point by asking Cane, "If a man is intimate with another man only once, does that make him totally gay?" Man will argue there is no clear-cut answer. Believe and trust that the God I serve does His best work when we are broken, confused, and completely messed up. But when we decide to come to our Heavenly Father in whatever state we're in or wherever we are in life, He receives us. The true Enemy of God (EOG), Satan, will saturate our thinking with shame, guilt, and no way out, but this is not God. "Come to me, all you who are weary and heavy burdened, and I will give you rest" (Matt. 11:28).

The world of entertainment has done a phenomenal job with mesmerizing stars and special effects portraying the enemies of God in favorable roles. Case in point: Pharaoh and Moses in the Ten Commandments was entertainment at its finest. Now for a reality check, that was a dark time in biblical history—countless innocent lives lost, generations of slavery, famine, and despair. God patiently asked a king over and over to obey him. Arrogance and disbelief caused this king to dismiss God and his messenger, Moses, as highly qualified magicians. It was not until death arrived at the king's doorstep that he surrendered. Unfortunately, this was a brief surrender.

Why do I refer to this movie? People refuse to believe a powerful and merciful God would destroy thousands of soldiers. Yes, they were following narcissistic orders, but more importantly they died believing in that charge. Throughout the Bible, God has destroyed individuals, families, ethnic groups, and entire cities. Regrettably, this is downplayed far too much. Most prefer to be reminded of a one-sided God who is loving, gracious, performs miracles, and opens the vats of prosperity. In my grounding, I desire to know an all-encompassing God to strike this balance of truth.

You will also hear statements like, "If you say God will reject what I feel in my heart, then I don't want to worship your God," or "That's what you believe, and everyone is entitled to their opinions." There is only one God, and He is the one true living God, and rejecting or strong obstinate opinions will not change the Word. I have faith, and I know God does not want anyone to perish, and this is why he gives us time and opportunity. "With the Lord, a day is like a thousand years, and a thousand years are like a day. The Lord is not slow in keeping his promise, as some understand slowness. Instead He is patient with you, not wanting anyone to perish, but everyone to come to repentance" (2 Pet. 3:8–9).

What a conundrum! Those we love, who are sensible, genuine, and thirsty-to-serve God people, purposefully decide not to worship God according to His teachings, but rather worship according to what's acceptable of their lifestyle. This high-stake risk of homosexual Christians negotiating a self-willed lifestyle in exchange for a belief that no condemnation is met in the afterlife is their logical belief at best. Many are in deep, loving, secure relationships, which makes it even more difficult to believe otherwise as well. Remember, most have not rejected God, only specific teachings. Our role in these volatile matters is to prayerfully consider the parable of the sower and the seed (Matt. 13:1–23).

A Personal Message to the Youth of the Kingdom Culture

Apart from the kingdom culture, you may hear, "Youth, be free to be yourself! Be who you really are! Be the best person you can be!"

I, too, will encourage these statements and add the precept, "In the will of God, youth, be free to be yourself! In the will of God, be who you really are! In the will of God, be the best person you can be!"

Freedom did not originate in America. It began with the Word of God. The EOG will attempt to convince you otherwise. Do not be deceived. "Now the Lord is the Spirit, and where the Spirit of the Lord is, there is liberty" (2 Cor. 3:17).

Yes, you will endure, perhaps, rejection, humiliation, and even isolation for standing against the EOG, but know this, God has you! Calling you a homophobic versus a hellphobic is lightweight. I'm not a homophobic, I'm a hellphobic. Why get in the game with the EOG when he has already been indicted by God? He can't offer you anything of real substance. Anything! By the way, it's not his to offer—he lies!

God's power and love are incomprehensible in comparison to what is offered by a free-fall culture. His freedom empowers, restores, forgives, and redeems your spirit into true peace and purpose. Align yourselves with God and be prepared for Him to guide you through limitless possibilities.

Lastly, don't become desensitized to sin. Allow me to clarify. It is a dangerous and useful ploy used by the EOG. When you become desensitized, the consequences seem less important. Case in point: if you see someone murdered on TV in real life, it's "OMG!" You see three people murdered, "That's awful." Now you see a dozen, it's "Wow, I can't believe that." Then someone murders an entire classroom, "This is where the world is going." Unfortunately, if there is murder on a grander scale, "What's for dinner? Where are we going to eat?"

All of the above murders are equal, yet our reactions and genuine feelings decline in sensitivity—as evil incrementally increases, it is positioning closer as a norm. This is a well-orchestrated plan by the EOG.

No, we can't cure all the world ills, but we don't have to turn our backs on everything either. Be diligent, watchful, and prayed up!

Please don't forget, the EOG has limited power, but *no* authority—only God has limitless power and authority.

Thinking on Things Above

Fellow New Testament Christians, please keep in mind we must adhere to the law of the land (howbeit most difficult to fathom at times), exercise Godly love, respect, and, above all, pray for family members, friends, and others who are struggling with homosexuality.

Saying "No! It's wrong!" is a desensitized statement. This approach lacks any conviction to even begin the process of intelligent dialogue. When was the last time you heard a sermon about the third heaven as it was revealed to John the prophet in Revelations? There are times when you must shift your point of view from dwelling on what is wrong to what will be right. Instead of negative browbeating, engage in conversations that speak about the things above as royal heirs. An example: "I'm choosing to believe God's Word will not return void, and I want to be there when He is living among His people. I do not believe in your sexual orientation, and as you've made a conscious decision, so have I." Most people are unaware that God will live among us in the third heaven. Meditate on what we hold to be true.

After the first and second heaven are destroyed, those lost are condemned to their second death. God will ascend down with the new city, and it truly will be glorious. There will be a great wall made of jasper with three gates on the east, west, north, and south and with an angel at each gate. The gates will be made of pearl. The foundations of this great wall will have twelve layers—the first jasper, the second sapphire, the third agate, the fourth emerald, the fifth onyx, the sixth ruby, the seventh chrysolite, the eighth beryl, the ninth topaz, the tenth turquoise, the eleventh jacinth, and the twelfth amethyst. Our tar and cobblestone streets are not worth mentioning in comparison to streets of a pure transparent gold. These precious stones designed by God will possess a quality not seen or known to man.

Perhaps, the sky is such an astonishing clear brilliance that we will actually see the solar system like never seen before. The air denoting any definition of clean and landscapes with who-knows-what colors unimaginably place me in a surreal state of being. As a believer, I anticipate all and much more of this splendor and glory. "Eye has not seen, nor ear heard, nor have entered into the heart of man, the things which God has prepared for those who love Him" (1 Cor. 2:9). I believe! God has only revealed a glimpse of His glorious plans for us, and our minds are just not capable of comprehending this supernatural mystery.

If you are discouraged and feel the battle is being lost, remember, it's not yours, but the Lord's. Meditate on this life after death and the new city, as I often do. This aging planet contains the remnants of man's less-than-best stewardship. In the book of Adam and Eve Chapter 1:2, "And to the north of the garden there is a sea of water, clear and pure to the taste, unlike anything else; so that, through the clearness one may look into the depths of the earth," with my miniscule imagination, I am envisioning surely something greater is being prepared.

Another source of strength for me are angels. I hold fast an angel, or angels were charged to my life the day I was born. Year after year, his presence and actions sealed this belief. I've honored my angel with a majestic name that I share with no one—a secret, if you will, for this time side of life. Our God is a God of order, and all of his creations are named, such as the angels of God. We name our beloved pets, even projects, storms, and events because it validates their significance to us, so I validated my angel. Of course, I do not pray to him, but I seek his help from time to time along with the Holy Spirit.

Be encouraged in the Lord! There is still power in the blood and in the name of Jesus. He is still on the throne and in absolute control. "For as the rain cometh down, and the snow from heaven, and returneth not thither, but watereth the earth, and maketh it bring forth and bud, that it may give seed to the sower, and bread to the eater: So shall my word be that goeth forth out of my mouth: it shall not return unto me void, but it shall accomplish that which I please, and it shall prosper in the thing whereto I sent it" (Isa. 55:10–11).

Remember, when Stephen was full of the Holy Spirit and made his powerful speech to the Sanhedrins, he looked up to heaven and saw the glory of God and Jesus standing at His right hand. "'Look,' he said, 'I see heaven open and the Son of Man standing at the right hand of God'" (Acts 7:54–60). They gnashed their teeth, and he was soon stoned to death after hearing the truth.

Early Christians neither had a voice nor both detailed covenants as we do today. By merely being a Christian, they were tortured, sawn in two, imprisoned, slain with swords, and had their entire households fed openly to lions. As stated in Hebrews 11, it was a "roll call of faith." Why then do some of us choose the position of a concealed spirit of fear and speak in selectively safe milieus?

Do not allow the eloquent speech or political meandering of non-Christians—or other Christians, for that matter—to challenge, distort, or dismiss God's Word on this subject. Must we always become disheveled in the miasma of popular frame of minds and culture norms, not keeping in mind the biblical accounts over and over of people not desiring to be in the will of God?

Imagine for a moment the ancient coliseums filled to capacity with enthusiastic spectators enthralled in the sport of flesh-tearing killings of Christians. Those atrocious acts were the popular frame of minds allowed by the governing law. However, the elevation of popularity was not God's law.

Every human being will experience eternity after death—either in hell or paradise. As free-willed spirits, once again, I will say I'd rather take my chances standing with the Word of God that it will not return void than with an "ever-changing with the times" culture. Perhaps, you are deeply troubled about your lifestyle, and your heart is compelling you to take a different path, but seek God's counsel first. God is always there to receive those who are seeking His face.

Let me suggest to those of you who are being consumed primarily by homosexual issues—I say, don't. Actively support politicians with legislation, organizations, entertainment, and individuals that correlate with God's Word, and at the same time be profoundly diligent to refrain from supporting politicians, organizations, entertainment, and individuals that are in deliberate objection of God's Word. The fact is that there is an overabundance of poor, homeless, hungry, mentally ill, abused, imprisoned, and hurting people who are in need of our love, service, and prayers for our lifetime.

Furthermore, violence, disrespect, or the mistreatment of homosexuals—or anyone, for that matter—is not conducive with the will of God, but this is simply man being led by his own spirit. If you are continually or actively engaged in these acts, stop. Please stop! Repent and begin anew! It's just that simple.

We are spiritual sojourners here for a brief passage, brief beyond our human comprehension. We travel this temporal journey with our satchel of choices—some inherit the wind, while other choices bless our souls, and *all* determine our divine destiny. A new world-altering issue could be positioning itself and requiring all of us to lay aside our nuisances and come together for the sake of this ever fragile planet.

Lastly, times past in my arrogant and rebellious state, I was guilty of emotional reasoning with God and not obeying His commandment to love others aside from their differences. Withstanding the fact, He patiently and unconditionally loved me in my weaknesses.

Emotional reasoning is natural, but let us be faithful and mature to move on into the spirit of the Word for guidance. Refrain from standing in the shadows of fear concerning the direction our current culture is heading. Trust Him! Be steadfast! Have faith to believe that the one true living God's love is more powerful than any powers of darkness or evil entity that befalls us. Let the redeemed of the Lord say, Amen!

> Walk in wisdom toward those who are outside, redeeming the time. Let your speech always be with grace, seasoned with salt, that you may know how you ought to answer each one. (Col. 4:5–6)

> And who is he who will harm you if you become followers of what is good? But even if you should suffer for righteousness sake, you are blessed. And do not be afraid of their threats, nor be troubled. But sanctify the Lord God in your hearts, and always be ready to give a defense to everyone who asks you a reason for the hope that is in you, with meekness and fear; having a good conscience, that when they defame you as evildoers, those who revile your good conduct in Christ may be ashamed. For it is better, if it is the will of God, to suffer for doing good, than for doing evil. (1 Pet. 3:–17)